THE GOSPEL OF CHAOS SERIES – BOOK ONE

FOREVER WILL END

Dom Brandt

authorHOUSE®

AuthorHouse™
1663 Liberty Drive
Bloomington, IN 47403
www.authorhouse.com
Phone: 1 (800) 839-8640

Published by AuthorHouse 07/16/2019

ISBN: 978-1-7283-1949-0 (sc)
ISBN: 978-1-7283-1951-3 (hc)
ISBN: 978-1-7283-1950-6 (e)

Library of Congress Control Number: 2019909918

Print information available on the last page.

Any people depicted in stock imagery provided by Getty Images are models,
and such images are being used for illustrative purposes only.
Certain stock imagery © Getty Images.

This book is printed on acid-free paper.

Because of the dynamic nature of the Internet, any web addresses or links contained in
this book may have changed since publication and may no longer be valid. The views
expressed in this work are solely those of the author and do not necessarily reflect the
views of the publisher, and the publisher hereby disclaims any responsibility for them.

ACKNOWLEDGEMENT

Special thanks Jess Millman for her editing and consultation services,
as well as Cheriefox/Fiver for creating a great cover photo.
You both are awesome!

Reader's Discretion: This novel contains graphic content, adult language and situations that may make some feel uncomfortable. It is for entertainment purposes only and by no means intending to offend based on ones faith, race, sexual orientation/preference.

PROPHECIES OF EVIL

L ong ago, during the age known as the First Era, a violent war—a war that threatened all life—was waged between humans, given existence by the One True Divine Creator, and the Apparitions.

These Apparitions had been brought to life by a special class of humans who, blessed with Divine-like power, forged a new people. Their intended role had been the maintenance of existential stability, but instead, many Apparitions grew corrupt with the power they'd been bestowed. Convinced that basic humans were incomplete beings, they defied their creators and sought the complete annihilation of humanity, envisioning a world order where they-themselves would be the Divines of a New Era.

But none could predict what many years of suffering, pain, sadness, and death would bring forth. A dense Aura of black and crimson. Sweeping across the lands, it destroyed all it touched. Any living thing—be it plant or beast or Man, no matter how gentle its heart—became corrupted, spiteful, hateful, murderous. The stragglers left abandoned in its wake called this Aura the only thing it was: Evil.

Those whose minds were wicked before Evil rose believed it a deity deserving of worship. They formed a cult under its name, and under that cult, raised an army dedicated to spreading the Will of Evil and bringing an era of endless despair, which they'd call The End of Days.

Most grew to accept this fate. Those who still held courage formed a resistance faction. Guided by the young and brave Apparition, Kiera— once a proud and beloved servant of the New Divines, turned against them—humans and rogue Apparitions united under the same banner. She forged a weapon capable of sealing Evil. Through a valiant effort, she and her allied Legion dismantled the armies of Evil, and shuttered Evil itself away so thoroughly, it could never threaten the world again.

An Era of Peace had come. Kiera was unanimously chosen to rule over the lands, and ensure the peaceful times would remain. It was during this time that she gave birth to a daughter.

No peace, however, is complete. This newfound era was threatened, too, when a mysterious figure allowed Kiera to read an ancient First Era scripture, its contents based on the Prophecy of Evil. What she learned revealed a series of events that would ultimately and inevitably destroy all creation. Everything Kiera had done had been a mere step in that inevitability, and—eventually accepting this truth—Kiera fell into a spiraling depression, shunning her allies and wanting nothing to do with her infant daughter.

Still a glimmer of hope emerged. One last shadowy figure appeared just long enough to give Kiera another piece of scripture: a torn parchment called of the Vanquisher of Evil. It foretold the rise of another, given the power to truly destroy Evil and bring an Era of Eternal Peace. As the Armies of Evil regroup, Kiera rallies her remaining effort into a search for this so-called "Vanquisher," and places her remaining hope in her only daughter to lead the next generation to destroy Evil once and for all.

CHE SLUM BOY

A wet finger jams itself into the sleeping boy's ear.

"*Geez!*" Kasen shrieks, falling from his ramshackle bed and landing in an irritated heap. Under a smattering of the intruder's laughter, he wipes a stream of drool from his chin and rubs his assaulted ear. "What's your problem, Vonnie?"

A moment ago, deep in this district of the disregarded, the young Apparition had tossed and turned in his slumber, unaware another had entered his ragged tent home. It was twenty-one years into the Era of Peace, after all. It was the age of *Evenrise*, the first Apparition civilization built after Evil had been sealed away, and—under the military protection of their Legion, named after Kiera's unified human-Apparition faction that dismantled Evil—most Apparitions slept more soundly than they had for decades.

Not all Apparitions, however, experienced the same peace. The leaders who had united under one roof (including Kiera, herself) had all since disappeared or been replaced. The entire human race had gone without a trace; Apparitions concluded the war had driven them into extinction. The new leaders passed strict social hierarchy laws that divided citizens based on wealth and worth. The Districts formed.

The District of the Higher Ups was made of noble-born, highly intelligent, and top-ranking military personnel. They used their position of power to bully and oppress the lower-class citizens with their laws. Below them—*way* below them—were the Commoners. They survived by selling goods and undertaking other labor. But with Higher Ups reaping the rewards of their hard work, most barely got by. Even lower than them were the residents of the Slum District—those regarded as Evenrise's most violent, feared, and hated citizens, and the biggest threat to the Era of Peace. A stonewall fence around the Slums ensured no one could enter. And, more importantly, it promised no resident could leave—unless they desired a headless body.

"It's morning," Vonnie finished laughing. She stood right over Kasen as he grumbled there on the ground. "You're going to be late, and you don't want to upset HER again, do you?"

Kasen groaned, but he knew he'd rather not.

Kasen estimated (for he'd no way to be certain) that he was just about thirteen years of age, and Vonnie eight or nine. Neither knew how they ended up in the Slum District. With no clue about who their parents were—or if they had close relatives, at all—they'd been fending for themselves. Their clothes were worn with all manner of gunk soaked in. They'd both grown out of their hole-filled shoes. (They were uncomfortable to begin with.) Their hair was messy with bits of debris stuck-in. They weren't as malnourished as most in the district. But Kasen wouldn't let his situation affect his sanity; he held on to the confidence that one day, things would change for the better. For him, for Vonnie, and for all residents of the Slum District.

As the two traverse the dusty Slum streets, they see other residents huddled in the alleys, comforting one another. Numbers mean protection, as any lone Slum-dweller is susceptible to theft or harassment by neighbors who lost their sanity. Abiding by this unwritten rule, Kasen and Vonnie stick close until they reach a familiar tent house, held together by tall totems and covered with blankets fit for royalty, its entrance guarded by two identical, flamboyant men. They sneer when Kasen and Vonnie approach.

"Look who decided to show," the first grunts.

"Late as usual," snaps the other.

"Jaun and Yaun. Identical, but thankfully not related," Kasen says.

"It'd be weird if they were because, you know...with you two." Vonnie presses her fingers together. The boys study her gesture with confused expressions.

"Know what?" Juan snaps.

"Obviously, they're jealous. They wish they had the kind of relationship we do," Yuan answers.

Kasen and Vonnie look at each other and shrug.

FOREVER WILL END

"Can we just avoid lectures today?" Kasen asks. Juan and Yuan had always surprised him with their banter.

"Then how about a reminder?" comes the deep voice of a woman from within the tent home. Juan, Yuan, and all those in the vicinity immediately bow as she steps outside.

She was nowhere near the condition of the others in the Slums. Her skin was smoothly moisturized; her dark hair was held in a long ponytail; she wore an elegant black and green dress, gold and silver bracelets around her arms; she sported diamond earrings. Today, her dark eyes stare menacingly at Kasen and Vonnie.

"Chantel," Kasen mumbles.

"Good morning, little thief. I'll start today by expressing my confliction with you. I give you shelter, food, a purpose, and all I ask is that you here on time. Or should I use a more 'hostile' approach in order for you understand?"

Vonnie lets out a soft peep when her eyes meet Chantel's dark gaze. Kasen quickly moves in front of her. Chantel never played by the books.

"There's work to do," she continues. "A longtime associate of mine has decided to no longer pay for protection, and is sitting on a heavy stash of debt. Er... resources. I won't explain what needs to be done, but if it doesn't get done, don't bother coming back, because even this brat won't be here. Juan and Yuan will make sure you do your part."

Stealing was the primary means of survival in the Slum District. Even kind-hearted individuals like Kasen had to conform. Chantel, on the other hand, did more than conform—she seemed to have her fingers in everyone's pocket, including those beyond the Slums, and if the Higher Ups hadn't already ruined one's life, Chantel was more than happy to contribute to the cause. Commoners would frequently be deported to the Slums if they couldn't meet the financial demands of their Higher Up overlords. They were allowed to bring whatever valuables they had, thus marking themselves as targets for thieves.

Kasen often accompanied Juan and Yuan on these heists, and along their route, they'd always see the same thing. Ruined homes, orphaned children, debris, and death. At the north end of the district sat a tall gate that separated the Slums from the rest of Evenrise; those who'd been recently deported established the area, waiting for guards to come around so they might plead for release.

"There's our target." Juan points to a heavy man sitting on a large supply of food and tools, a fellow currently busy chasing off thieves with a long knife. Kasen's mouth waters just looking at the spoils. He's always known stealing was wrong, but he won't let the real Slum District starve.

"Look at that stash." Yuan's eyes beam. "It'll last weeks."

"More like seconds, with your stomach," Juan snaps.

"I swear," Yuan flirts back, "you know me more than I know myself."

"I know," Juan softly replies. The two passionately lock eyes. Kasen snaps his fingers—which wakes them from their trance, but also throws them right back into rolling those eyes at him.

"Oh, right—*you're* here. OK, then listen up. This fatso has additional supplies inside his home and he periodically makes checks. Problem is: there's only one of him, and he can't check both at the same time. When he checks on his other valuables, that's when we'll go—one-at-a-time to not look suspicious—and you take as much food as you can. When you hear a whistle, you've got about two seconds to get the hell out of there, so stay low and pay attention."

As the man goes to check his additional supplies, Juan quietly makes his way over to the stash, and stuffs all he can into a small bag. When Yuan sees their target exiting his home, he sharply whistles and Juan quickly returns before he's noticed.

"Lady Chantel will certainly reward me," Juan brags.

"Oh, please," Yuan boasts. "Watch this."

Tired from going back-and-forth, believing he'd chased away the would-be thieves, the Commoner takes a short rest. Yuan makes his move, and like Juan, he's able to loot a fair amount before being whistled to return.

"More than you," Yuan proclaims.

"Show me." Juan swipes at and misses Yuan's bag.

"For Lady Chantel's eyes only," he says, their fidgeting again turning into play.

Kasen heaves a sigh. "Whenever you're done, guys."

"Look at you, only smart-talking when Lady Chantel isn't around,"

Juan snaps. "There's nothing special about you. Why does she even keep you around?"

"Just whistle, and save *that* for a different time." Saying so, Kasen stealthily makes his way to the stash.

"What the hell's he talking about?" Juan snaps.

"You know, we don't *have* to whistle," Yuan suggests, and two giggle at the thought.

As Kasen sneaks toward the stash, he gazes upon the towering Slums gate. On the other side: a world where you don't have to live in constant fear, a world away from Chantel's wrath. To save Vonnie's life, and many others, he was to be Chantel's *little thief* for the rest of his own.

As he fills his bag, Kasen wonders if anyone on the outside even cares about the Slum District. If Evenrise was built to maintain peace and unity, then why do only a few select Apparitions get that experience? If only he could show them how much pain and suffering they've endured.

His dreaming's interrupted when he feels the sharp edge of a knife poke the back of his neck.

"Drop the bag, thief." Kasen feels the Commoner's hot breath against the back of his neck. He spots Juan and Yuan giggling maliciously as they zip around the corner. Kasen obeys the command and raises his hands.

"Fucking Slumfolk. I would've killed you on the spot, but I've got some dignity—unlike your kind."

"You're right to be upset. I'm sorry I stole from you, but people are depending on me to bring something back. I wish I had a better choice."

"And you trust those oblivious lovebirds to help you?"

"I don't trust them at…wait, how do you know them?" Kasen was allowed to turn and face the man without succumbing to harm. He stared into the anger and sadness of the eyes looking back at him.

"That bitch, Chantel." The name brings him to the verge of tears. "My family on the other side has little to eat because of her. Why should anyone be intimidated and threatened by Slums? I could kill a hundred of you and no one would care. It's terrible to see kids forced to live this way, but I can't let you goons continue to harass me and my family."

The man readies to sink his knife into Kasen, but Kasen is faster; he quickly collects a handful of muck from his shirt and tosses it, hitting the man's face and mouth. Kasen quickly grabs his bag and darts down the street.

He hears the man's cry has he flees: "If I see you again, I'll kill you!"

Vonnie expresses her joy when she sees Kasen coming around the corner to Chantel's tent. Juan and Yuan, on the other hand, are obviously wondering how he managed to get out of his situation alive.

"Wasn't expecting you back," Chantel says.

"Here I am." Kasen dumps his catch over Chantel's feet. "Freshly stolen, the way you like it."

Juan, Yuan, and Vonnie stare wide-eyed, mouths open.

Chantel softly chuckles. "I'm thankful. So thankful I'm letting you brats starve tonight while we feast. Now, if you are done making an ass out of yourself, get out of my sight."

Juan and Yuan laugh, watching Kasen and Vonnie leave empty-handed.

When sunset comes to Evenrise, Kasen can usually be found sitting atop the only tree in the district. It's a withering thing, but has held firmly all these years, even during harsh weather. The tree stands tall enough that climbing it offers a glimpse of the world beyond the Slums.

"What did you do that for?" Vonnie complains, clambering up next to him. "We haven't eaten in days and I was looking forward to tonight."

Kasen unveils a small jerky piece and a loaf of bread, which Vonnie greedily snatches. She gobbles down the jerky piece and tears through a good chunk of bread. It is only after that she realizes this meager food was all he had.

"Sorry," she hiccups, offering Kasen what little is left.

"I'm not hungry." Kasen's growling stomach says otherwise.

"You've been staring beyond the Slums for a while now, Kasen."

"Yeah. Maybe one day we'll get to see it all up close."

"Slumfolk aren't allowed to leave the District."

Kasen hated being reminded. "That's what I don't understand," he argues. "Isn't Evenrise supposed to be a civilization built on peace? But to them, it's like we don't even exist."

"We've managed for people who don't exist," Vonne softly replies.

"For how much longer? There must be some way to show them we aren't the bad people they claim we are. Someway. Somehow. We can be free of Chantel, and no one will have to live like this anymore. I'm going to find a way."

Kasen knows Vonnie isn't a fool. No Slum would dare challenge or cross Chantel. Regardless, Vonnie never stopped believing in him—a part of her truly did, at least.

Unknown to either of them, their dreams of freeing the Slum District would come much sooner than they anticipated.

SACRED BORN

The same night Kasen and Vonnie imagine life on the other side of the Slum District, in the Uncharted forest regions of the North, a group of ragtag Apparitions traverse the dark woods.

These Apparitions belonged to a group known as Feral: scattered units formerly of the Armies of Evil, now broken off into small squadrons of their own. So long as the Uncharted Region—a land of dense, dark forests and deep caves, misty bogs, and mountains—remained uncharted, it likewise remained difficult for civilized Apparitions to root out where the Feral took shelter.

Having received word of an intruder in their territory, these Feral are en route hunt them down. They halt at the sight of a young girl—around Kasen's age—in deep meditation under the moonlit night.

The Feral peer at her through the shrubs. "She's been like that all day," one observes.

"This is our territory," shrieks another. "Let's gut her and be done with it."

"That's not how to please the ladies, boys," counters the most charming and toned Feral of the bunch. "Look how the moonlight illuminates her skin, her blond silk hair. This is every man's dream."

They seem to agree, and with that decided, emerge from the shrubs to surround her.

"What's a petite young lass such as yourself doing alone in the dark scary woods?" Most-Charming asks. She remains perfectly posed amid the Ferals' grunted chuckles. "It isn't safe or smart for young ladies to wander off into the Uncharted Region. My friends here eagerly want to do all sorts of things to you, and I'm your only way out of this. So why don't you come with me, lovely?"

FOREVER WILL END

"Power," the girl speaks. Her eyes open, revealing a light blue. "I'm the first and only descendant of Sacred Aura. I've been gifted a power it took my predecessor most of her life to accomplish. However, my potential has yet to be achieved."

The Feral exchange looks.

"Are you sure she's your gal?" one asks Most-Charming. "She seems rather coo-coo."

"None of you could comprehend." She rises to her feet. "Each day I'm tested. No—limited—against opponents far inferior to me. Will there ever come a time where my limits will truly be tested?"

"OK, girl, you've babbled enough." The charming Feral attempts to grab her.

Quickly, the girl draws a sword and slashes him deep across his waistline, and he falls, inner fluids pouring out. Before the other Feral can react properly, the she performs a spinning motion that cuts down all but one, leaving her surrounded in mutilated bodies. The last Feral catches her cold stare and lets out a frightened peep before fleeing into the dark.

"Stupid little girl," he spits, glaring behind him. "She'll pay dearly once I inform the boss."

But before he can make another yelp, a second figure dashes in and decapitates him. His head rolls next to the young girl's feet.

"Power alone isn't all I need," the girl contemplates, allowing the loose head-blood to creep toward her feet. "It's also a symbol that represents that power. The Sacred Blade. A weapon forged that has no equal. A blade that I'll pry from YOUR hands."

At that threat, a majestic, tall, and light woman reveals herself from behind a thick tree. She wears a white and blue combat outfit, similar to the young girl's, and her platinum blond hair radiates beautifully under the moon. Her eyes are an empty dark blue.

This is the once-courageous Kiera—the same leader who sealed Evil away decades ago and, with the Divine power she called Sacred Aura, brought peace to the land. Kiera now passes her knowledge and abilities to her only daughter, Ashli, who has grown spiteful of her mother over several years of strict and severe training. Ashli desires to become the strongest Apparition alive.

"Is power all you seek, child?" Kiera's tone of voice shifts dramatically.

She speaks as though all hope has been lost—as if there had never been a pleasant exchange between mother and daughter.

"If I wasn't born to surpass you, why was I born, at all? This training—no—preparation to become Ruler of Apparitions can't be for anything else."

"What have you become?" Kiera stares into her daughter's cold blue eyes. "All you feel is anger and hate. Has your quest for ultimate power consumed you?"

"It's anger and hatred of you. No matter how stronger I become, I always fall short of your expectations. But once I've slain you, and claim what's rightfully mine, then maybe some of that anger and hate will fade." Ashli assumes a stance. One that leaves no blind spot.

"You may try."

Once Kiera assumes her stance, Ashli attacks immediately.

Even the full force of Ashli's swordplay skill isn't enough to best her mother—Kiera easily dodges every swing, and Ashli, irritated, only increases the ferocity of her attacks.

"A blade filled with anger and hate will never reach me. Focus, child," Kiera instructs in the middle of battle.

"The last thing I need is your advice," Ashli snaps while still rapidly swinging.

"You're not ready to claim the title of Ruler," Kiera states. "To exceed beyond your potential, you must learn to cast away your weakness."

"I have no weakness." Ashli's rage swells. When her next attack misses, she receives a rib-breaking palm thrust that sends her careening into a nearby tree. In pain, Ashli rises, spitting out a mixture of saliva and blood.

"Bitch." As she swears under her breath, Ashli's limbs go numb, and she plops to the ground, her body refusing to respond to her.

"My daughter. You've many weaknesses. Until you overcome them, you will remain hindered. Lie there and think on it. You won't be moving for a while."

Ashli curses her mother once more before she disappears into the darkness.

This is hardly the first time Ashli's been so humiliated in combat. Kiera often preached on how strength is more than a name and title.

Regardless, Ashli would never give up on her conquest of becoming strongest. She knew one day she'd best her mother and become ruler.

Ashli wakes from her stupor just after sunrise. She is able to move again, but every part of her aches and the earth around her is trembling.

Footsteps—hundreds of them—heading in her direction. Feral appear from the thickness of the Forest in droves. They form ranks as a tall man with his woman clutching at his wrist walk between them. They peer at Ashli.

"This the little brat that's been killing my guys?" he growls.

"Indeed," answers Kiera, following the Feral pair. Mother and daughter exchange cold stares. "Perhaps you'll learn something, most likely not. You're running out of chances."

"Oh, she doesn't have a chance," the Feral leader barks at Kiera. "Now get lost. This brat is in desperate need of tough love." Kiera leaves Ashli to their mercy.

"How many?" Ashli simply asks.

"My entire squad of three hundred and fifty," the Feral leader boasts.

Ashli sighs with disappointment. "I won't learn anything from this."

"All right, boys, make it painful!" the leader orders, and the Feral shout as they charge at Ashli. Ignoring the soreness in her limbs, she draws her sword and holds her ground.

Ashli impales her first victim and dodges a slew of others' attacks before she cuts them down, as well. Under Kiera's instruction, she'd become proficient at determining how to use the environment to her advantage. Open fields, dense forest, narrow and confined spaces—most are utilized as the battle rages into the night. Heavy rain begins to pour as the forest becomes littered with mutilated corpses. The Feral leader and his woman can only listen to their men being slaughtered.

"That bitch set us up; this girl's gonna kill us all." The frightened woman clutches tight to the Feral leader, riddled with anxiety as their entire army is slain in a matter of days. He knows he is soon to be next.

"Shut up," he roars. "I can't think until you shut up."

She shakes his arm when things turn quiet. "Wait. Listen."

Ashli appears from the darkness, her clothes, face, and hair soaked with the blood of those she'd slain. She walks with an agonized limp, looking though she'll collapse from exhaustion at any second.

DOM BRANDT

The angry Feral leader pushes his frightened woman off him. Taking out his sword, he charges at Ashli. It's a fatal mistake on his part—she splits him nearly in half.

The Feral woman kowtows, and pleads for her life.

"Show mercy, I beg you. That man chose to wage war against you, and now I'm a widow with three children. I was only following my superiors, but I see that it's been you all along, my lady. Spare me, and I swear to serve you for the rest of my days."

Ashli drops her sword. Prompts the Feral woman to believe Ashli's accepted her offer.

"My lady, you're most kind." the woman cries. "I swear on my children you won't regret this mercy!"

When she stands, shaking with relief, Ashli punctures her hand deep into the woman's abdomen.

"A coward doesn't deserve to die honorably, much less serve under me." Ashli rips her hand away, and the Feral plops to the ground.

'A complete waste of time,' Ashli thinks. *'What could anyone learn from a handful of cowards and thugs?'*

Something heavy hits across her face. She rolls along the wet earth.

"Damn you," Ashli hisses, knowing well her assaulter is her mother.

"Falling short, as always," Kiera sighs. "You think of battle as a prize to be won, and never a learning experience. Sometimes slaying your enemies isn't the smartest choice."

"Are you sympathizing with those fools? If you didn't want them to die, you shouldn't have sent them after me. You've only yourself to blame."

"Perhaps so," Kiera agrees. "However, they were a kind that follow the strongest. Had you convinced them, you could've used them to defeat me. Well, at least you might have stood a chance."

"You talk too much," Ashli snaps. "You'll be number three-fifty-one."

"My daughter, this night won't end well for you," Kiera replies, before she engages her child in yet another skirmish.

Though Ashli is a power-hungry, short-tempered mass-murderer, Kiera would put the fate of all existence in her daughter's hands when Evil once again descends upon the world.

WHIMSICAL DEVIL

As Ashli slays several hundred Feral, the storm reaches its climax. Another girl—not much younger—runs, scared for her life, from a pack of vicious beasts. She trips over a tree root and flops into a ditch of mud. The beasts surround her small hole, giving their prey no chance of escape.

A lightning strike above the trees is enough to spook them off for now. The girl, drenched heavily with mud, fights to her feet. She sticks out her tongue at the last of the beasts as they disappear into the forest.

"Stupid assholes," she snarls, the twangy accent of the Uncharted tribes thick in her curse.

This unfiltered girl is Kika. Underneath her layers of mud lies the pale texture of animal hides, her rough-hewn clothing a marker of most Apparitions who dwell in the forest regions. Her wild dark curls sprout in different directions above unnatural violet eyes.

Kika belonged to a unique Apparition race—the Bizarre—who, unlike their human-resembling *Norm* cousins, take on a variety of animalistic traits while retaining human shape and size.

How the Bizarre species even came to be had always been a popular bit of folklore among Apparitions. One of their Divine had loved animals and nature so much, said the myth, they transformed themselves into a mythical creature. As a creature, the Divine traveled the world and listened to the prayers of the animals. After hearing them all, this Divine reshaped many animals to have a human-like body, to know how to speak the human tongue, and to possess the human intellect. The Divine had spent so long as a creature, however, they'd forgotten what they had looked like before, and couldn't return to their former self. Instead, they decided to merge their essence with nature, becoming one with it.

DOM BRANDT

When the newly-transformed animals revealed themselves to the human populace, they described this merger as the most bizarre phenomenon they'd ever witnessed. The *bizarre* term seemed to stick, and they've been defined by it since.

Kika's Bizarre trait was that of a Southerlands Devil—the stout black badger-dogs who have for many years held a notorious reputation for their tremendous strength and nearly unstoppable fits of rage. Despite the anger-fueled reputation of the Devil Bizarre, however, Kika had never been power-hungry. She didn't desire the thrill of the kill like a Feral, nor did she have uncontrollable fits of rage. Kika, with all her questionable mannerisms, was too free-spirited to be on the battlefield.

Kika climbs from the mud ditch; awaiting her at the top is a straggling beast.

"Aw, shit," she curses in the last instant before the creature pounces on her, sending her back into the ditch again. It sinks it teeth deep into Kika's neck and rabidly shakes; she gasps in horror.

Until—for some unknown reason—the beast releases her. It begins to yelp and whine as its teeth break and fall from its mouth. Its bottom jaw snaps, and dangles, and finally its head splits open, plopping lifeless over Kika.

As if nothing happened to her, Kika pushes the beast off, showing no signs of injury.

"Ew, I can see your brain…brains? That's gross."

Though Kika wasn't a fighter, she wasn't by any means incapable of doing so. Through it remains an unorthodox practice, the Southerlands Devil Bizarre have managed to turn their own bodies into lethal weapons. Any foolish or reckless attack against them could shatter the attacker's limbs. (Keep in mind: the process to achieve this effect is unorthodox.)

Kika, bloody death averted, continues playfully along through the rain-soaked forest—until something hits her hard enough to make her to fall to her knees, knocking the wind out of her, leaving her groaning in pain. She looks fearfully at the hulking dark figure that towers over her.

"Thought you could escape?" His voice comes deep and intimidating. "On your feet now, or feel worse pain."

The assailant is her own father, Malik, and this isn't the first time he struck his daughter hard enough to kill several men. For Southerlands

Devil Bizarre to obtain their unnatural physique, they have to endure several years of immeasurable physical pain and abuse, and Malik shows no mercy, even to his innocent daughter.

When his child fails to heed his warning, Malik wraps a palm around her face and lifts Kika off the ground. "If anyone's the stupid asshole, it's you."

"Screw you." For her insolence, she is struck even harder, in the exact same spot.

"Nearly twelve years, and I'm still finding it hard to believe you're my kin," Malik growls. Kika makes a painful noise as he tightens his grip around her head, muffling a smart comment that can't escape her hand-sealed mouth.

Despite her lineage, Kika has little to no resemblance to her father—or even the Devil trait.

"If I'm hurting you, just say so," Malik laughs. But his fingers clasped over Kika's mouth grow lazy, and separate enough for her to chomp down on one. He violently throws her to the ground.

"Conniving little shit." Malik stares at the blood oozing from where he was bitten, surprised to see Kika getting to her feet after all she's endured.

"I was trying to say: All you ever do is keep yapping. Devil this, Devil that, but you're just some punk-ass bully. If that's the only way to get off, then keep your dumbass powers."

With a bodily gesture, Malik emits a force of energy that sends Kika flying into a tree.

"Believe it or not, it pains me to put you through this." He watches his daughter hacking on the ground. "I won't blame you for hating me for the rest of your life—hell, I wouldn't even be surprised if you end up killing me for what I'm done to you—but I hope one day, you'll understand that what I'm doing is preparing you for something much worse. I won't ask your forgiveness, but what I am asking from you is something I can't ask from anyone else."

As Ashli endures a night of constant defeat and embarrassment, Kika endures abuse. Still yet-to-be-known to these young ladies, however, is the truth: With their combined powers, and with the Vanquisher—whoever it was—they were to one day face, and ultimately destroy, Evil.

365ᵀᴴ DAY

The night's storm clouds disperse to make way for the sun. Droplets fall from leaf tips and pelt Ashli as she lies below them. She shields her eyes from the brightness. She doesn't remember passing out on her own free-will. Bruises and battle-marks cover her arms and legs. She hurts even worse than the days prior.

Using anything in-reach for support, Ashli hauls herself along the forest floor, coming eventually upon a stump hidden under a thick cluster of ferns. Several hundred carved markings litter its bark: one for each day that went by.

"Three hundred sixty-one, two, three... four!" Excitement rushes through Ashli when she engraves the three hundred and sixty-fifth marking. This is the 365ᵗʰ Day. The one day she is permitted to spend as she pleases, so long as she remains within the established territory of her training grounds.

"Your rules are stupid, Mother, and so are you," Ashli says as she breaks that very rule and travels farther into the forest.

The environment around her grows lush and livelier. Critters play around the trees; birds sing in the branches. But it is the rustling lone bush that gets her attention.

"Are you there?" Ashli whispers harshly.

"...No," answers the young girl hiding within.

Ashli creeps closer. "Why are you hiding?"

"Why aren't you?"

"Come out," Ashli chuckles.

"Alright." Kika reveals herself. She, too, stands before the forest in a body tattered with bruises and cuts. "You know, after you get past the first dozen, the next hundred aren't so bad."

"You shouldn't talk like that," Ashli replies.

"Well, it's not like you look any better. But still..." Kika smiles with delight—one Ashli returns. "It's good to see you again, super pal."

"You know what this means... tag, you're it!" Kika taps on Ashli before scurrying away.

The two spend their day playing children's games, splashing in the stream, and interacting with the woodland critters. Their struggles of the three hundred and sixty-four days prior fade from their memories.

It was an unexpected encounter—at first. During a time when Ashli was younger and less experienced. She was fleeing from a Feral group that were too much for her. Her mother hadn't come to her aid that day, so she ended up running to the current spot she and Kika were playing in now. What she found there? A younger Kika—crumpled on the ground, crying out to her father for help. A colossal Feral stomped through the forest in Kika's direction, strong enough that it was knocking over trees.

Ferals soon surrounded the two girls. The colossus raised a foot over Kika, and stomped down hard enough that the earth trembled. Ferals cackled with pleasure as the stomper warned Ashli she was to die in a worse fashion.

But then the warnings scattered into cries of pain—that deadly foot had broken, and now dangled. Leg bones popped one after the other until the Feral's pelvis shattered and, finally, its spine snapped.

The giant Feral timbered. Not wanting to share the same fate as their comrade, the others retreated.

It was an odd introduction, but the girls had formed a close bond in the years since—and every 365th day, they'd spend their time together.

Late afternoon: the sky becomes a mix of orange, yellow, and pink. Ashli and Kika end their fun by enjoying the sky spectacle from atop the trees.

"Best. Day. Ever." Kika stretches her limbs. Ashli smiles heartedly and nods.

"Hey Ash..." Kika nudges her best friend with a finger. "Has *she* ever mentioned why she does what she does? This sucks." She groans. "My asshole of a father keeps babbling that I must become fiercer than he is. But even if I did want to... I can't."

"We're their sole heirs. They need us to carry on their legacy," Ashli replies.

"But when we do, or whatever. Will we still be able to have fun like this?"

"We'll always be friends. I promise," says Ashli. They sit quietly as the sun sets and stars begin to fill the night sky.

"I should return before my mother notices I'm gone," Ashli says. "Remember to keep track of the days."

"Fine. Goodbye, super pal." Kika watches Ashli climb down.

The latter makes a hasty return to her training grounds. It is only when Ashli finds the coast clear that she sighs with relief. Seeing Kika is the only way for her to get through the next three hundred and sixty-four days.

"You're unusually chipper." Ashli's heart drops. Kiera had been posted on the branches above her daughter all along.

'How long has she been there?' Ashli wonders as her mother jumps to the ground. Before she can even mutter a smart-alecky remark, Kiera reveals a glowing blue sword.

The Sacred Blade—the same one that sealed Evil away. Just the sight of it puts Ashli in hypnosis. The long-awaited symbol of proof she needs to rightfully claim the title of Ruler is just in reach.

"Tonight your true test begins. The knowledge and skills you've acquired over the years will determine if you're worthy to succeed me."" Kiera sticks the blade into the earth. Ashli is too fixated on it to hear her mother. The blue hilt and chrome steel—all perfectly edged for a supreme warrior. "It's a fitting blade for a Ruler, wouldn't you agree?"

"We both know who that is, so hand it over," Ashli snaps.

"Patience, child. You will have what you've sought after. There's one thing left that stands in your way."

"You." Ashli draws her sword. "Just so we're clear, I don't intend to show remorse."

"To acquire the Sacred Blade's power and have the ability to conjure Sacred Aura, I had to sacrifice something that I not only deeply cherished, but also what I inferred was my weakness. Now you must make that same sacrifice."

"Do I need to spell it out for you, Mother? I have no weakness!" Ashli shrieks.

Kiera smirks. "Then performing your task at-hand shouldn't be any trouble."

Out of the darkness hulks the Apparition man—and, clutched in his palm, the battered and beaten Kika.

Kiera notices Ashli's face turn ominous.

"This is Malik, the Bizarre who rules these lands, He's given us permission to use them for your preparation to rule. When his daughter, Kika, comes of age, she'll inherit them. Or she was to, until Malik declared her a waste of life."

Ashli gives Kiera a snarling stare.

"To assume we weren't aware of your actions in our absence? You must really take me for a fool. You may have fallen short of expectations several times before, but this is the first time you've disappointed me."

"Waiting 'til now to discipline me?" Ashli scoffs. "I can never take you seriously."

"Ha. You'll need ice for that burn," Kika hisses, even through the pain of her father's grip upon her.

"How about this one?" Malik breaks Kika's arm, and she cries out in fresh agony.

Ashli temper flares. "You son of a—"

"Attempt anything, and her pain will be tenfold," Kiera warns.

Her fury feels like she's trying to hold back a storm with her hands. Ashli only manages to remain still by looking to her friend. "Kika, are you alright?"

"Well, my arm got snapped like a twig, and I might be bleeding internally; other than that, I'm fine. How are you?"

"Quiet," Malik barks.

"You'll do exactly as I say," Kiera tells Ashli. "To prove you're Ruler of Apparitions, that weakness you harbor must be cast away. It's quite clear this wretched girl stands between you and absolute power. You'll take the Sacred Blade, and end her life."

Malik laughs. "Hear that, brat?" he whispers in Kika's ear. "Your miserable life will be over soon."

"And I was worried for nothing," Kika replies.

Ashli feels conflicted, uncertain, vulnerable—powerless. She can't look her mother in the face; she doesn't want anyone to see her this way.

"I won't. Please let her go," she begs, voice trembling, but only for a second. "I'll never see her again, I swear."

"Pathetic child," Kiera coldly notes. "If you have no weakness, then prove it. TAKE THE SWORD."

Ashli flinches at her mother's bellow.

"Ashli," Kika says softly. "Don't worry about me. Just take the sword," she shouts, "and chop off their damn heads!"

Ashli moves. Slowly and steadily, she goes over to where the sword is planted. Her mind races for a way to get Kika out of this situation, but knows Mother would already be ten steps ahead. She's within an arm's length of the Sacred Blade. Ashi reaches for it. Kiera and Malik watch with anticipation, as all Ashli has to do is wrap her fingers around the hilt.

Retracting her hand—and herself—from the sword, Ashli stops. Her head hangs in self-pity and defeat.

"I'll find another way. Punish me however you will. Take your sword, and go to hell." She coldly stares into the eyes of her mother.

"Ashli no!" Kika cries. "What about your promise? You said we'd always be friends." Ashli can't look Kika in the face.

"Worry not, child," Kiera replies. "You can be friends. In life..."

Malik punctures Kika through her back and out through her stomach. Ashli lets out horrid gasp as Kika chokes.

"...and in death."

"Best—friends—always." Kika weakly reaches out to Ashli, until her arm dangles back to her side. Malik tosses her limp body to Ashli's feet.

"Kika?" Ashli whimpers. Kika doesn't move or respond.

'This is a bad dream. *Wake up, already.*' She repeats this phrase—bad dream—in her head several times over, until the harsh reality began to settle.

"You must realize now that you were never capable of becoming Ruler. I refuse to waste any more time on you. I leave you with nothing to show for your unworthiness."

As Kiera grabs the Sacred Blade, Ashli clutches around her arm, hurls Kiera overhead, and slams her to the ground. Ashli yanks the Sacred Blade and strikes down at her mother, causing the earth to erupt with dirt and dust.

When the cloud clears, it reveals Kiera—still alive, barely scuffed. A single spot on her forehead leaks crimson.

A light blue Aura radiates from Ashli; her eyes flare with the same hue.

"What's wrong with her?" Malik shields his eyes from the bright glow.

"She's unstable. I'll solve this matter," Kiera says, and Malik disappears into the woods.

"I've had enough of you!" Ashli shouts. Feeling the Sacred Blade's power making her stronger than she imagined.

"It's as I feared. The Sacred Blade's beyond your comprehension."

"Are you blind, Mother?" Ashli snaps. "The Sacred Blade is mine to wield. I'll use it to cut you down, and assume my role as Ruler."

"I only see a disobedient daughter that needs discipline," Kiera calmly replies.

"You've spoken your last. Now die!"

Ashli charges Kiera with furious speed. She leaps into the air and brings the full force of her attack down onto Kiera. Kiera holds her position as the assault becomes too close to dodge without sustaining serious injury. The blade makes direct contact—before it shatters into nothing more than dust particles.

"My daughter, allow me to put it into words you'll understand." Ashli's glow disperses; her energy is rapidly draining. The particles gather and reform the blade in Kiera's hand, and she impales Ashli's heart.

"You'll never become Ruler, nor will you wield the Sacred Blade."

Ashli feels undying pain as Kiera pulls the blade from her. She falls to her hands and knees, clutching her wound as blood seeps through.

"You battle without purpose, each attack motiveless. You tread on a path to nowhere. Your foolish obsession with power has hindered you for too long, and it is why were unable to save both yourself and your friend. As your breath withers, think of how this outcome could've differed if you thought about more than a fancy blade and title. Even if—by some miracle—you recover from this, the Sacred Power will be lost to you. Farewell, my daughter."

Ashli watches her mother disappear into the night. With her remaining strength, she drags herself next to Kika's corpse, and sobs over her.

"I'm so sorry. I was weak, I've always been. Please forgive me." Ashli lays her head on Kika, just as darkness overtakes her.

Ashli.

She hears Kika calling her. Is this death? Absolute darkness? *Ashli,* Kika calls again. She can't respond—she doesn't want to. She can't beg Kika to forgive her for being too weak.

"ASHLI!"

Ashli opens her eyes as if springing back to life. It is a new morning—the skies are clear above where she lies on the open grass.

She looks left, right, then up, and sees Kika standing over her.

"Kika?" Ashli sits up.

Kika smiles and waves. "Hiya."

"I don't understand. You were. WE were."

"Yeah, we got the crap killed out of us last night... I think. Maybe we're immortal."

Ashli wants to believe Kika, but feels weaker since she woke. Kiera's words echo in her memory: If she survived, she'd lose the power she had.

"We have all the time in the world. Whatcha wanna do, super pal?" Kika asks.

Though weaker, and sure of it, Ashli won't let a setback stand in the way of her becoming the strongest Apparition. She'll have to find a new power. A power greater than Sacred Aura, and when she does, she'll repay her mother dearly for years of humiliation and defeat.

Getting to her feet, she sets off on the terrain.

"Ashli, where are you going?" Kika follows after.

"To surpass my mother in every aspect. She told me of the civilization she ruled in the east. That's where I'll begin my path."

"OK. What should I do?"

"Where I'll go, I'm sure to engage in many battles. You'd be safer and happier if you remained here."

"So you're just gonna leave like that? Fine. I'll find a better friend," pouts Kika, turning her back, but Ashli continues walking, and it doesn't take long for Kika to roll her eyes and follow again. "Dammit, Ashli. I'm going, too, but only because that's what I want to do."

"What about how you feel about fighting?"

"I know what I said," Kika snaps. "But you can't forget that promise—about always being friends. So if you're gonna do something lame, then I'll watch."

"Thank you for understanding."

"So, with that established... race ya there." Kika takes off.

"Kika, you're going to wrong way," Ashli calls to her.

High above the forest glade, a mountain outcrop gives Kiera a good view of her daughter and Kika beginning their journey.

"Ashli, my daughter. You were too strong for your own good. If you had followed the path to self-glory, Evil would've taken hold of you. Your power will remain sealed until you've learned what power like ours is truly used for."

"Are you sure they're ready?" Malik stands beside her, watching.

"If Kika is your daughter, she was born ready." Kiera turns to her lover. "It took everything I had to seal away Ashli's power. My own power is fading. I don't have the strength to face Evil again." Tears fall down her cheeks. "All we've fought for. All who gave their lives to save this world— it was all in vain. How foolish we were to think that sealing Evil would be enough." Kiera chuckles at her incompetence. "Evil will descend on these lands again. And we prepare by passing our burdens and failures onto our own children... who'd sooner end our lives."

"There's still time." Malik wipes the tears from Kiera's face. "We'll do all we can until that time comes. I believed in you and I'll believe in them. If we can't find the Vanquisher, they surely will, and they'll destroy Evil once and for all. Most importantly: No matter what happens, I'll never stop loving you. I want to see you smile once more."

He pulls Kiera to him and she rests her head on his chest. Even false hope is sometimes comfort enough. She doesn't have the heart to tell him she may not live to see Evil destroyed.

"My daughter, your true test: Succeed where I've failed."

ONE LAST JOB

for disrespecting Chantel, Kasen had been deprived of food for days. Normally his mornings begin with Vonnie waking him by practical joke, but he had gotten himself up today, and headed to Chantel's tent alone.

The streets and alleys of the Slum District seem to him less populated than most days. *'What's Chantel scheming now?'* Kasen wonders as he enters into her home.

Juan and Yuan sit at a breakfast table, intimately sharing cake, while Chantel lies sprawled over her chair, sipping wine and dining on fruit fed to her by her servants.

"Want a piece?" Juan slides a mouthful of cake into Yuan's mouth, which he overdramatically savors.

"No thanks," Kasen declines.

"Little thief, will we ever get along?" Chantel stretches lazily. Kasen responds with a glare. "You're such a badass. Most thank me for all I do for them, even if I give them a pile of shit. You, on the other hand, would be the dumbass to refuse it."

"Or be the smart one to shove it down your throat."

Annoyed with having to dismiss their cake time, Juan and Yuan quickly and aggressively restrain Kasen for his insolence.

"This Slum gig of mine is only a temporary thing," Chantel continues. "Taking what I want, when I want is all good fun, but this hellhole makes obtaining things on the outside very difficult. And there's something I've sought after for years now."

"Can't help you there," Kasen replies.

"Don't sell yourself short. I honestly can't think of anyone more qualified. Some of my informants sent word a Legion Commander carries an ancient black sword of extraordinary value. Be a lamb and fetch it for me."

Kasen laughs. "You're joking, right? That's impossible, and how am I supposed to get past the gate?"

"Leave the icky parts to me. If you miraculously complete this task, you can retire early from thievery."

"I'm telling you, it can't be done," Kasen argues.

Chantel doesn't budge. "And I'm telling you to get it done."

"Well, too bad. I'm not doing anything that dangerous." He pulls himself out of Juan and Yaun's hold, and proceeds to leave Chantel's tent.

"Understandable, little thief... but how will you explain to the brat girl why she died today?"

Kasen whips back to Chantel. A dark grin spreads across her face.

"Hadn't occurred to you why she hasn't shown up yet?"

"Where is she? If you've done anything, if she's hurt at all..."

"You already said you wouldn't do it, so what good is she to me after I've snapped my fingers?" Chantel presses her fingers together.

"Wait!" Kasen mumbles something foul under his breath. "I'll do it, but first prove to me she's OK."

As if it were magic, Chantel displays a glowing image of Vonnie, unconscious and ensnared in vines.

"For now, at least," Chantel says. She gives Kasen a folded sheet containing his instructions—where to go, the name of the target carrying the black sword, and Vonnie's location. "If you retrieve the brat before you retrieve the weapon, I promise you'll be soaked in her entrails. Get going, little thief. Time is not on your side."

Kasen hurries out of Chantel's home.

Reading her handwriting is a difficult task on its own, but from what he can decipher, the first step on the outline is to wait by the gate. By the time Kasen arrives, nearly the entire population of the Slum District is already gathered there.

"You again." The same Commoner he stole from a few days prior appears in front of him. Kasen remembers his heavy breathing. "Because of you and the loverboys, I gotta pay protection to that Chantel whore."

"I'm sorry." Kasen doesn't look into the large man's eyes.

"I'm only doing this because she promised to get me out of this dump and I can be with my family again. So that means you're going to do exactly what I tell you, got it?" Kasen nods, and the man continues. "On rare occasions, Legion guards make rounds along the gate. We'll cause a loud enough uproar that they'll hopefully be fooled into opening up. Once they're in, we'll split them apart and push ahead to create a short window for you to slip through. That's your one and only chance and there's going to be blood, so no fucking up."

An hour ticks by like a lifetime as Kasen and the other Slums resident wait, one of them peering through the small holes of the gate. Finally, they spot three guards walking the perimeter. With a signal to the group, the Slumfolk shout, and slam their fists upon the gate. Sure enough, their rioting infuriates the guards enough for them to unbolt the lock; they shout and hit the rioters to silence them, but it only amplifies the chaos. Overwhelmed by their numbers, the guards are quickly pushed apart.

"Now!" The large man shouts to Kasen. And he quickly weaves his way through the crowd.

The guards draw their swords and begin hacking at Slums. They scatter, but by this time, Kasen has already successfully snuck past.

He breathes the cleaner air of the Commoners District. The Commoner people are hard at work in their various labor duties, so they can meet the grueling demands of their Higher Up superiors. The withered trees that hold dead and dying branches are few and scattered.

Remembering his tight schedule, Kasen reads Chantel's next set of instructions, and follows the outer pathways to a private gathering where the target will be.

"Evenrise. My mother ruled this civilization." Ashli and Kika stand outside the main gates of the city.

"What's that smell?" Kika covers her nose. "Are we really going in there?"

"I never concerned myself with why she abandoned her Ruleship," Ashli adds, determined. "But I'll prove her wrong about my capability. To put it clearly: Yes, we are really going in."

"Outsiders! Come no closer." Archers positioned over the gates aim their crossbows at the two girls.

"Check it out, Ashli. That talking guy's talking to us." Kika points.

"Evenrise is a civilization of purity and order. Unless you bear the Legion insignia, return from whence you came. This is your only warning."

"I'll come and go as I please." Ashli stands her ground while Kika becomes distracted by some insects crawling along the ground. The archers take position, albeit poorly. Some visibly shake and sweat—unskilled and undisciplined soldiers.

"Then you'll be executed." The commanding officer signals to the archers. "Ready...aim...!"

"I command that you lower your weapons this instant," orders a handsome and charming young man. The kind of man women want to show off—his oiled hair, hypnotizing eyes, and all-around physique imposes upon those around him. The guards immediately salute.

"L—L—Lord Edwin!? How unexpected."

"You intended to execute these unarmed ladies? And poorly, by the looks of these men."

"My Lord. Our laws state."

"I know what they state," Edwin sharply replies.

"Forgive me, sir."

Edwin redirects his attention to Ashli and Kika. "I couldn't help overhearing the name Ashli. Ashli the Sacred Born?"

"Whoa. You're like the greatest guesser in the world," Kika points out.

"That name alone is famous. No other Apparition shares it. Evenrise has eagerly awaited your arrival. Open the gates at once!"

Ashli and Kika gaze upon the Higher Up District of Evenrise. Its citizens are dressed elegantly compared to the Commoner and Slumfolk. The air within the district carries a pleasant fragrance; its streets bustle with children and adults. Edwin gives Ashli and Kika the tour of the city—or at least, the city he wants them to see. They end their trip in front of a grand military institution.

"Behold: Legion Academy," Edwin announces. "My father and his father worked tirelessly to build a civilization of morality over one of savagery. There's still much work to do, but I believe we're well on the right track. As luck would have it, here arrives no finer example of an individual."

A tall man equipped in a full bronze and black armor, with Legion's banner caped over his back, steps in. A Commander. Omar. One of Legion's best soldiers, not known to hold back under any circumstance. He was also a man shrouded in mystery, as very few knew what he looked like underneath his helm, including his most trusted subordinates.

Edwin politely gestures to him. "I thought you'd be eager to see the Sacred Born for yourself. This is Ashli and her friend, um... yeah."

"Sacred Born Ashli and her friend." Omar's voice is an old and grumbling one. "I'm sure Lord Edwin has welcomed you with proper hospitality. But if there's anything more I can do to make you feel welcome, you need only ask."

"Enough of this pointless squabbling." Ashli grows tired of walking and talking. "I've come here for the sole purpose of becoming stronger. Or have I merely wasted time?"

"You'll have to excuse her. She'd rather fight things than not-fight-things," Kika says.

"Then look no further." Edwin points to a long cluster of withered trees along the river. "A fiendish creature has managed to make its home along the water and has infected the area it occupies. We'd prefer this issue remain unknown to the public, if it isn't too much trouble. I'll even lend you my sword. I mostly wear it for show, but it should silence the beast." Edwin hands Ashli a sword that looks not entirely unlike the Sacred Blade. She accepts, but only because such a proposition is sure to get her away from this place and these people for a few moments.

'He smells weird.' Kika studies Edwin. 'Wonder if he already knows.'

"Pardon me, Lord Edwin. My presence is needed for another banquet." So saying, Omar takes his leave.

As Kasen nears his destination, delectable smells making his mouth water, his stomach growls fiercely, and the need to eat subsumes him into a trance to follow the smell to the source.

Until, that is, he hears an all-too-familiar giggling behind stacks of straw.

FOREVER WILL END

Juan and Yuan are all over each other on a straw bed they made. The two repel themselves from each other once they see Kasen has caught them.

"What are you guys doing?" Kasen shrieks.

.

"We—We're minding our own business." Juan wipes off the straw caught on his clothes.

"And making sure you're not gonna to screw us," Yuan snarls. "Er... I mean, screw Lady Chantel. Wait! I mean—"

"What we're saying is if you SCREW this up, your little brat's friend's good as dead."

"Still keeping it a secret? Well, it's not my place to judge, but if Vonnie's hurt at all, 'screwing' won't be on my mind." With that said, Kasen continues on, and out.

"What the hell's he even talking about? He's such a pain in the ass," Juan snaps.

"Not as painful as you." Yuan taps Juan's nose.

"You two don't change, even after all these years." Chantel reveals herself, sitting cross-legged on top of the straw stack. Juan and Yuan kneel before her.

"Lady Chantel, your asshole of a little thief is nearing the target as we speak," they report in sync.

"Those Legion bastards. Always taking what doesn't belong to them. I should thank them for keeping my sword safe after all these years, once it's mine again. Maybe unleashing a bit of hell on this pathetic city is the best way to show my appreciation."

"Hail, Lady Chantel. The greatest of Apparitions," Juan and Yuan cheer.

The banquet assigned to Kasen is nestled near a river. Approaching carefully, he observes from a safe distance. The armored commander who towers over the rest of them supposedly carries the sword Chantel wants.

"Citizens of Evenrise, I bring great news," Commander Omar announces. "Just a few hours ago, the Sacred Born arrived to our glorious city. We've been blessed with the True Ruler who will guide Evenrise to an even brighter future." The Higher Ups clap, and Omar nods under their appreciation. "Wonderful news, indeed. But we've gathered here for more than just an announcement." His audience chuckles—in a sinister sort of way. "There's been a slight change in today's merriment. Due to a minor obstruction, the Slum girl we've acquired now has a chance of survival. The Sacred Born has taken it upon herself to slay the fiend lurking in the woods."

"But will she kill it? That's what matters here," a Higher Up complains.

"I've a better idea. Anyone be willing to wager the Sacred Born does, in fact, kill the Slum child? It'd make today's entertainment more entertaining, to say the least."

"If she's going to be our Ruler, she better."

"If she doesn't kill it, at least Commander Omar will."

The Higher Ups commence with their bet as to whether the Slum would be killed by the creature, the Sacred born, or Omar. Kasen knows in his gut they are referring to Vonnie. He won't let her be their entertainment.

Bravery and stupidity together take a hold of him, and—not caring about getting Chantel's sword anymore—he emerges from the shadows to confront the Higher Ups.

"You people are disgusting," Kasen shrills into the crowd. Attention immediately shifts from the bet to the filthy mess of a young boy now standing amongst them, seemingly from nowhere. "Wagering on someone's life like it's some game?"

"How are we the sick ones when you look like you've taken a bath in animal shit?" a Higher Up questions.

"That's my friend's life you're betting on," Kasen snaps back.

"So that makes you a Slum varmint, as well." Omar asserts his way through the citizens. His height alone gives Kasen chills. "How'd you get passed the gate, Slum boy?" he barks.

"My—my friend," Kasen stutters, ignoring his question. "I'm getting her back."

"Commander Omar, kill this degenerate little shit," a partier suggests, and his Higher Up company express their approval.

"In the name of Legion and all law-abiding citizens of Evenrise, I will end your miserable life. May your death serve as a reminder of what happens when one forgets their place."

Omar draws a pure black chrome sword. It's futile for Kasen to try and defend himself; he has little choice but to close his eyes tight as the blade swings down upon him.

Nothing happens.

It is a phenomenon—unexplained, unexpected. The sword reflects off Kasen, escapes Omar's grip, and falls by the Slum boy's feet.

He capitalizes on the unexpected turn of events, grabbing the sword and hurrying into the woods. As he flees, he loses his instructions, but knows Vonnie has to be somewhere close. The farther into the woods Kasen travels, the darker it grows, and the trees around him begin to decay, hundreds of thick vines coiled around them.

Vonnie. He manages to spot her, dangling in a cluster overhead. Kasen tries to free her, puling at the vines with all his might; as if coming to life, the vines pull Vonnie further into their grasp.

"Give her back!" Kasen hacks and pulls harder at the vines. His persistence awakens a vicious plant creature. It peers at Kasen with its salivating mouth, and snaps.

"Give her *back!*" he insists again, both furious and frightened. The creature responds with a vine whip across Kasen's face.

He growls as he gets to his feet, wiping the red smear from his mouth. But—as if appearing out of thin air—he finds a strange girl has taken his position. She doesn't seem to notice him; her attention is on the creature. But Kasen definitely notices her.

"You're no Feral," she notes, observing the twisting mass of vegetation as it hisses and drools. "But that's the only difference."

As if it took some sort of offense, the creature shrieks at the girl, and uses every vine at its disposal to ensnare her. Effortlessly, she severs her way free and leaps into a dead branch above.

"I'm Ashli, Sacred Born, destined Ruler of Apparitions, and you are merely a forgotten memory." She brings her sword down upon the creature, splitting it in two. Its inner fluids gush over the ground, and its numerous vines wither away.

Vonnie is freed from her vine prison. She falls backwards as if feinting.

Kasen, panicking, takes her into his arms, sighing with relief after hearing Vonnie's soft breaths.

"Dammit," Ashli spits, pulling her blade out of the seething mass. "I'm definitely weaker. One swing of a sword and a leap, and I'm exhausted. Just wait, Mother. I'll surpass you soon enough."

"Th—Thank you." Ashli turns to the sound of gratitude, coldly glancing at Kasen. The sword he carries clearly catches her eye.

"The sword," she barks. "Hand it over."

Not giving Kasen time to think, Ashli swipes it from him.

"There's something unusual about this weapon," she murmurs, examining it. Kasen blinks helplessly at her with Vonnie still limp on his lap. "What's an ordinary boy doing with a sword like this? It's no Sacred Blade, but it'll do."

"Wait. You can't just take it," Kasen protests.

"You're right. I should've killed you first, then pried it from your fingers." But as Ashli readies to attack him, the black sword disappears from her hands, and reappears into Kasen's. Another phenomenon.

"You've slain the beast. Well done, Sacred Born." An approaching voice interrupts them. Somewhere during the brief battle and the confusion of its aftermath, Omar had appeared. "I hope this troublesome boy wasn't troublesome."

With Vonnie in his arms, Kasen flees.

"That boy's a Slum," Omar informs her, even as he crashes through the scrub. "Petty thieves, murderers, and other lowly scum of the earth. If you'll return to your friend, I've got to deal with damage control."

'*What a strange boy,*' Ashli thinks, as Omar pursues Kasen, and she returns to Kika.

Kasen is lost in the woods. For a moment, he even believes he's escaped, but the Commander is in hot pursuit.

Using his great power, Omar pounds a fist into the ground, creating a shockwave that topples Kasen and Vonnie over.

"Return what you've stolen, and maybe your death will be slightly less painful," Omar forebodes. Fear, anger, and guilt fill Kasen's mind.

He was too weak to save Vonnie from Chantel, from the creature, from Omar, from anyone. He stands frozen in-place, awaiting his fate.

A figure drops down between them.

"Chantel?" Kasen is astonished to see her, of all people.

"Commander Omar. Where's the time gone?" she simpers.

"Chantel? When did you decide to crawl out of your hole? No matter; I've got bigger priorities at the moment. Hand over that Slum boy, and let's call it a draw."

"Come now, Omar, we both know how this will turn out. Unlike you, I remain loyal to my cause."

Kasen wants to speak, but before he can, Chantel gives him an instruction sheet on how to return to the Slum District.

"Typical of you to screw up, like always. Get moving before I reconsider his offer."

Heeding Chantel's words, Kasen takes Vonnie—and, shaken, they return to the Slums.

"Hello," Kika happily says when she and Edwin see Ashli emerging from the forest, fresh from her hunt.

"My lady. Now that you're settling in, I thought we'd take a moment to discuss your future prospects as Evenrise's Ruler."

"I don't need your treatment," Ashli bristles. "I will only prove that I'm worthy to rule, and if that means enlisting in this charade of a military, then so be it. Perhaps I'll learn something, but I highly doubt it."

Edwin's face twists in discouragement, but he remains composed. "Of course. I couldn't think of a better way to prove your worthiness. Two days from now, I'll hold a recruitment exam. From there, we'll see where your future lies." He throws Ashli a set of keys. "Feel free to use one of the academy's guest suites. We expect great things from you, Sacred Born." Edwin lightly bows before taking his leave.

"Ashli, don't you think you're overdoing it?" Kika asks. "That guy was so boring, and he smells weird. Let's go have fun like old times."

"My mother, your father. They're still alive," Ashli counters, her voice itself a chill in the perfumed city air. "They made fools of us. You should want them dead more than I do, and I won't find any solace until they are. It's time for us to grow up, Kika. Once we achieve strength beyond theirs…we'll kill them with it."

As Ashli walks past, Kika thursts out her tongue.

"You're no fun anymore," she mumbles, before following after.

A thin rope dangles over the stone walls of the Slum District, just waiting for Kasen to climb up.

He and Vonnie are hoisted over by the large man and a few other residents. Many Slumfolk lie slain through the streets, many more seriously injured. Kasen looks around at the devastation—so many lives ruined, all for some sword.

"This better be the last time I deal with you Slums," the large man bickers. "The second that wench pardons me, I'm taking my family and getting the hell out of this damned city."

"I'm sorry for what I did, truly," Kasen swears—dismayed at the smell of his neighbors' blood and the senseless ruin around him, he means it, too. "I knew Chantel was cruel, but I believed even she had limits. I won't make that mistake again. I'll find a way to make this right. For everyone who's been affected by her."

"Your tramp of a boss wants her new toy first thing in the morning," he grumbles, and leaves.

Kasen carries a still-unconscious Vonnie to an old standing cottage. Withered flowers remain on its doorstep from the last time Kasen was here.

"It's been awhile," he says softly. "I wish I could say something like, *'Things have been going great since you left!'* But that's not true. People are dying, and I'm too weak to do anything about it. My hope that things will get better has run dry. I'm tired of being unable to do anything about it. Please, I need a sign, anything at all."

The black sword appears in Kasen's hand and he angrily throws it at the ground, hoping it'd break. But the thing simply reappears in his hand again.

And he slowly realizes there may just be a way, after all.

"Ugh. Kasen? Where are we?" Vonnie's voice surprises him—she stirs awake on Kasen's bed.

"Safe," he assures her. "For now."

"Juan and Yuan. I remember them taking me somewhere. Someone gave them a lot of supplies—cake, mostly. Then everything went dark."

Kasen clenches his fist. "Chantel used you to get me to steal some sword, but I was too weak to rescue you myself." Vonnie jumps when he slams the same fist onto the bed. "If it wasn't for that girl, we wouldn't be here, at all. Many died today, and I was too weak to do anything. Chantel's gone too far."

"What can we do?" Vonnie wonders, voice meek. "We don't have anything that can stop her…"

"Doing nothing is worse. We'll just have to try, is all. This entire system needs to end. I have to join Legion and find a way to stop it."

"But Kasen. The law—"

"I don't care about Evenrise's stupid law. This city was built to unify us, but it's only been one law after another—and none of them do anything but crush people like us. I may have found an answer." Kasen shows Vonnie the black sword.

She stares at it in awe. "What kind of sword is that?

"Whatever Chantel's after, she must need this, so I just won't let her have it."

"But Kasen. Why are you standing up to Chantel *now*?"

"I had the opportunity to escape the Slum District once. Along with a few good friends from before. They found you in the alleys around that time. You were gravely ill, and we believed you wouldn't survive the night. I really wanted to escape, because I knew wouldn't survive if I stayed. But I wanted to save you more, because even in a place like this, there can be some good. I stopped thinking about myself, and what I wanted. It wasn't fair that only a few of us could go free, while the rest were left to perish. The entire district needs to be free, treated fairly. For that to happen, I have to become stronger for everyone."

Vonnie nods. "OK, Kasen. But you can't do this alone. I'll have your back as much as I can."

Heist complete, sword stolen, day done, Chantel returns to her tent with her henchmen at her side and silk in her hands.

In the comfort of her home, she undresses before the two boys. Juan and Yuan turn away from her bare flesh in a mix of respect, disgust, and discomfort.

"I couldn't imagine you with lady parts," Juan whispers to Yuan.

"I could. I just wouldn't find you interesting anymore," he replies.

"That Omar," Chanel cuts, either unaware of their conversation or simply uninterested in caring about it. She pulls the silky material over her head with a *tsk*. "No manners at all. Just leaves without saying goodbye. Just *ugh*." Dressed in her nightgown, she plops on her seat. A servant offers her a glass of wine that she sips and savors.

The large man barges into the tent. "I got your Slum slave pet past the gate. Now hold your end of the deal and absolve me of my debts."

"Oh, Otis, dear. It's been a long day; can you bitch at me another time?" Chantel groans.

"My name's Sampson."

"Really? You look like an Otis. Anyway, Otto, listen..."

"You listen, stupid bitch." Sampson smacks Chantel's wine glass from her hand. "You've harassed me and my family long enough. You'll make good on your promise, forgive my debt, and never bother me or my family again."

Chantel folds her hands, and crosses her legs. "Alright, you win. Your debts are forgiven," she says as casually as a breeze.

"Just like that?"

"Just like that," Chantel agrees.

"Er... thanks?"

"Make sure you say goodbye to your family before you leave," she adds, and with a curl of Chantel's finger, everything changes.

Sampson's wife and two sons are pushed into the tent by Chantel's other henchmen.

"What the hell's this?" Sampson demands, but a darkness deep within his eyes suggests some part of him already knows.

"Who do you think was paying fpr their upkeep while you kept being an uncivilized member of society? Don't worry. They'll only work 'til I no longer need them."

"Over my dead body." Sampson pulls a knife from his pocket. "Back your goons off my family, or this is going in you as many times as it has to for you to shut up."

"Oliver. Samuel. Whatever your name is. I make it very clear to my underlings that they only live for as long as I need them to, and now that you've done all you could, well..."

Juan steps behind Sampson, and—grabbing his knife-holding hand—he gouges Sampson's throat. His family screams in horror, and he turns to see them one last time before collapsing. They crumble over him and weep.

"He did say over his dead body," Chantel chimes in. "So now that you understand how things work around here, you can start by getting his fat ass out of my home. We've still got a lot of work to do, and I have the perfect role for you, Ms. Widow."

DESIRING CHANGE

Kasen wakes up the following morning more awake than he's ever been. Today, Chantel's tyranny over the Slum District would end.

"Are you sure about this, Kasen?" Vonnie asks him once more.

"If we don't stand up to her now, we won't ever." With his decision made clear, Kasen and Vonnie proceed to her home.

It would be a long time before the Slums recovered from the casualties of their staged rioting. Kasen had helped pile those who'd been slain overnight. Since the District lacked proper equipment to bury or burn the deceased, the bodies were more to likely rot where they piled than have a proper burial ceremony.

Kasen and Vonnie find Chantel, Juan and Yuan, and a small crowd of Slum residents gathered outside her home. Among the crowd: the widow of Sampson and their two boys.

"Ah. Little thief," Chantel sings. I knew I could count on you to get the job done. Your years of serving have finally paid off. Now, hand over the sword." She snatches it from Kasen as soon as she sees it.

It fits so naturally in the palm of her hand, she thinks, mesmerized by the feeling.

"Residents of the Slum District!" she announces. "Too long we've endured the aching pain of oppression by this so-called glorious civilization. They've isolated us because they're so frightened of those who are slightly different that they'd rather believe we don't exist. Like the monsters in their nightmares. It's time we show them how frightening the monsters in their nightmares really are. A terrible omen will fall upon this city, and only I can save you from its wrath. Residents of the Slum District, you've suffered long enough. Join me in an era without Evenrise, and become your own Rulers." Chantel raises the sword overhead.

"Glory to Lady Chantel!" Juan and Yuan cheer.

"With this blade, the seal will be broken, and the Prophecy of Evil can be fulfilled—GAH!"

She shrieks when a clawing sensation shoots through her, causing her to drop the sword. Her hand and arm are covered with deep bleeding cuts. The black sword retakes its place in Kasen's hand.

"No. It's not possible, you shouldn't be able to." Chantel's voice trembles in anger. "What have you done?!"

"Guess it didn't like you," Kasen retorts.

"This isn't a joke," Chantel cries, fierce, voice cracking. "Do you have any comprehension about what you're holding?"

"I wasn't planning to give you this sword in the first place. Everything that's happened to us—our pain and suffering—is because of you. You exploit us, steal from others, and now you're selling us to Higher Ups."

A gasp came from the circled Slums. More gather around the crowd to see what's going on.

"Everyone, please listen," Kasen directs to the crowd of bystanders. "We don't need Chantel to survive. If we learn to work together, fight together, we can become better. I'm choosing now to fight for our freedom and become a Legion soldier. I won't let this drive us to insanity, and will make sure people like them never threaten your livelihoods again."

Chantel claps. "Truly a motivational speech. I'm assuming you helped him prep, brat?"

"You brought this on yourself, Chantel," Vonnie shoots back.

"I remember back when you first scurried into my home, little thief. You begged me to save these people from an illness. In my head, I only thought of how much of a little bitch you were to sell your life away— that one day, you'd surely end up doing something that'd annoy me too much." With a quick thrust of her hand, Chantel clutches Kasen's neck, and lifts him into the air. He fights to break free, but Chantel's hold is locked and secured. Vonnie is swiftly restrained by Juan and Yuan.

"In fact, you may be the most annoying shit I've ever dealt with," Chantel marvels, but her anger is plain. "If I go, the Slums die, end of story, so why don't I do them the favor of killing you now, before they all starve?"

Kasen's face turns pale, his eyes bloodshot. But before he fully asphyxiates, she releases him. He plops to the ground, panting to regain the air he lost.

"Lady Chantel!" Yuan frowns, perplexed. "Why did you stop?"

She sighs. "Seems I made a miscalculation. Apparently he's formed some sort of connection to the sword. If I kill him—as much as I really want to—any number of things might happen with the sword. The most frustrating of them being: it could disappear completely. Maybe," she ponders, eying Kasen as he gasps and paws at his already bruising throat, "your ambition of joining Legion isn't such a bad idea. And I suppose I owe you for retrieving the sword, at the very least."

"Don't let them scare you like this, my lady," Juan blusters. She ignores him. "You don't need some sword to accomplish your goals, anyway."

"You'll get Vonnie and me past the gates. This time without any casualties," Kasen manages, but it's difficult to sound confident while he's holding his burning throat in his hands. "And you're done enslaving the people of the Slum District?"

"If it'll help you all sleep better, then fine. You—lady with the two kids," Chantel snaps, flicking a finger toward the widow. "Could you kindly escort our beloved heroes to the gate?"

"I thought I said no—"

"I heard you the first time," Chantel snaps. "C'mon, lovebirds. Let's find neighbors who actually appreciate all I do for them."

Juan and Yuan are still gathering Chantel's luggage when Kasen and Vonnie take their leave.

'Surely they have their own way of getting out of the District,' he thinks as they follow the widow to the gate.

"How will she get us past?" Vonnie whispers.

Kasen shakes his head, neck still stinging from where she'd throttled him. He knows he'll have a furious mark by morning. "When it comes to Chantel, it's never good. Be ready."

"How will you save the Slum District?" the widow asks as they walk. Chantel had left a terrible mark on her life, too—but this wound wouldn't heal with ice and cold water. "You know these people won't last long without her."

"I know. I promise to find something," Kasen replies.

"I'll make sure he keeps that promise," Vonnie adds, before the trio arrives to the gate. The widow taps it.

"Who's there?" snarls a voice on the other side.

"I've brought the two wishing to cross," the widow says, "in exchange for the agreed payment offered by Chantel."

The gate creeks open. Two creepy-looking guards with rough faces and stout bodies peer at them.

"Hurry up, Slum rats."

"Er. Thank you, sir," Kasen stammers as he slips through. Vonnie, however, stops mid-step.

"What was the payment?" she demands.

The guards snicker in response.

"Me," the widow answers, with tearful eyes. "I'm her last laugh."

"And how could we refuse a damsel in despair," one laughs as the other grabs her by the shirt collar, tearing it. She stumbles, but does not resist. Kasen lurches forward reflexively, trying to pull her free of them, but is pushed away.

"Please keep your promise and save my sons," she pleads, as the guards close the gate.

Kasen bangs against it, demanding they rescind the deal. It doesn't budge.

A step away, he can feel Vonnie's eyes on him, watching for something to do.

"Let's hurry, Vonnie," he tells her, finally, swallowing a hard lump down his sore throat. "They're counting on us."

They follow the signs that lead to a side entrance of Legion Academy. It's disconcertingly easy; the Legion patrols don't even seem to care. Even the guards positioned at the entrances seem more interested in loitering than guarding. Upon seeing Kasen and Vonnie approach, however, a few spring into formation.

"Not another step closer, citizens. These doors are for Legion personnel only. Turn back or we'll be forced to use force."

"You said force twice," a comrad scolds.

"We want to become Legion soldiers," Kasen says. The guards look at each other with puzzled expressions. It isn't everyday a pair of kids in rags asks to join.

"Come back when you have better jokes."

"We aren't going anywhere." Kasen stands firm—but with no other option clear to him, ends up begging. "Please. All we want is a chance."

The guards place their hands over their weapons. "Turn back or be arrested for trespassing on Academy grounds."

"What now?" Vonnie whispers at his side.

'Maybe there's another way in,' Kasen thinks. 'I bet we could—'

But before he can finish the thought, the black sword unexpectedly appears in his hand.

The guards draw their weapons. "Drawing a weapon on Legion personnel's a serious offense."

Kasen can't find the words to explain what happened.

"Then allow me to carry forth the punishment." Omar—in his trademark armor—struts down a path along the perimeter.

The guards salute.

"Crossing the gate illegally, twice. Invasion of privacy, theft, now this? You've committed too many crimes to live."

"I'm not a criminal," Kasen snaps back, but the black sword is still petrified there in his hand. "You took my friend against her will, so I got her back."

"She was purchased legally by Evenrise customs. So don't think on your life I'll allow Slum filth through these doors." Omar draws a great sword.

"It's not my life I'm worried about. It's those in the Slum District."

Omar shakes his head. "All those crimes, and you come here wishing to join Legion? The only thing you'll join is the afterlife."

Kasen grabs Vonnie and they dive-roll away as Omar brings his sword down upon them.

"Hold still, you little punk." Omar swings wildly at Kasen several times more. Deprived of food over the past few days, Kasen's energy is already low; he's tiring within minutes. "You're well out of your league, Slum boy. What makes a criminal think he's the right of joining Legion?"

"I promised to fight for the people of the Slum District. I intend to make good on that promise." Using the remainder of his strength, Kasen attacks. The black sword hardly leaves a dent in Omar's armor.

"That's the best your promise can do?" Omar seizes Kasen's head in one mighty palm and hoists him. "This is how you inflict pain." He jams his fist into the center of the Slum boy's stomach. For the second time in a day, the air forcibly escapes his lungs.

"Let him go," shouts Vonnie, hitting at Omar's leg. He kicks her away.

"If you're going to steal a sword, then at least have the capability to use it. Or is that too much to expect from a Slum?" Omar tosses Kasen over to the guards. "Teach him what happens when you disrespect the laws of Evenrise."

Kasen isn't entirely sure what happens next. Life blurs. One guard holds him while the others take turns punching. As the haze of pain descends on him, he's only certain of the sound of Vonnie's furious shrieking.

"Why? Why are you doing this?" she yells, but receives no response.

"Let's see him." The guards hold up a beaten and bloodied Kasen at Omar's command.

"Still sure about keep that promise, Slum boy? I'm surprised you're still conscious after that ass-kicking." Omar pries the black sword from Kasen, and turns his attention towards Vonnie. "You first."

Kasen squirms frantically, but his attempts only win him the renewed attention of the guards; they pummel him once more.

"I—I'm not afraid of you." Vonnie stands her ground against the towering Omar. She knows the risks of entering the skirmish, but she won't let Kasen endure it alone.

"It's not like I enjoy taking a child's life. But however unjust they may be, I'll always uphold the laws of Evenrise."

A polished boot kicks Vonnie to the ground. She cries out after Omar plants his foot over her head.

"I'm the one you're after," Kasen wails.

"Take a look at that boy over there. Because he, you, and many others will die." He aims the black sword at the back of Vonnie's head.

"Omar!" Kasen screams louder.

"It's OK, Kasen." Vonnie smiles at him from beneath Omar's foot. "We got to be free. Even if it was just a moment."

Kasen yells at the top of his lungs—and, suddenly, time comes to a screeching halt.

Vonnie, Omar, the guards are frozen in-place. The black sword releases itself from Omar's grip and hovers above him, radiating a green light.

"I've felt your overwhelming desire since the very moment you encountered me, young Apparition." The sword speaks with a deep and soothing voice. *"I've long yearned to be wielded again by a kindly soul. Accept me, and I'll bestow upon you the power you need to fulfill them. The only question you need to answer is: What IS your desire?"*

Kasen grasps the sword between his fingers, and immense energy fills him. He's always known his desire, and as time resumes its normal pace, the guards holding Kasen are blown back by a burst of green aura erupting from him.

"How'd he get the sword back? How's a Slum able to conjure Aura?" Omar growls. "No, it's that sword—he's drawing it from the sword. Maybe he's not an ordinary Slum boy, after all."

The guards recover quickly to surround Kasen. "We'll take care of this criminal, Commander."

"After he blew you all away? Get out of the way, grunts. This one's mine to destroy." The pounding of Omar's heart writes anticipation all over his stance. He's dying to see what this Aura can do.

And attack he does—only this time, he's repelled. The guards are astonished to see one of Evenrise's strongest fighters so unceremoniously deflected. Omar merely laughs at the thought of it—of a fight between a Commander and a Slum boy.

"This is more like it. Nothing in life is more enjoyable than a battle where any outcome's possible."

"Fighting to save lives isn't a game," Kasen snaps.

"I beg to differ," Omar replies as a dark yellow Aura rises from him. "I'll admit this has been entertaining, but I need to end our time together before I become sympathetic towards a criminal. Your little boost won't be enough. Time to die, Slum boy."

The fighters charge, their swords clash. Both struggle to overpower the other, and indeed, it's Omar who seems to be winning.

"My desire," Kasen grits, "is to change everything. And I WILL."

With a mighty shout, he cuts through Omar's blade and into his armor. The force of Kasen's blow knocks the Commander back several feet, and he crashes to the ground.

FOREVER WILL END

With his opponent defeated, the green aura surrounding Kasen fades away, and the black sword disappears. He collapses to all fours in exhaustion. Vonnie has to help him even remain on his fours.

"He defeated the Commander?" The guards look in disbelief as their superior lies motionless.

"Kasen, is he—?" Vonnie's sentence is interrupted by Omar's loud groan. The Commander hauls himself back to his feet, blood leaking from the gaping rift in his armor.

"Is he indestructible?" Kasen watches in dismay; he doesn't have the strength to fight again so soon.

"I've served Legion a long time. I've defeated foes who were convinced of their own immortality. I thought this world had run out of suitable fighters—until some no-name Slum bastard comes along," Omar huffs, pointing, hand red with his own blood, "and not only draws out the power of that black sword, but also does quite a bit of damage with it."

"I get it. I was stupid to try," Kasen pants. "I'm sorry, Vonnie. I tried as hard as I could, but it wasn't enough."

His moping stops when Omar bellows laughter.

"You may have literally achieved the impossible, and damned if I'm going to let that potential be wasted." He tosses Placement Exam Invitational guest passes at Kasen and Vonnie's feet. Commanders would often hold them to personally invite their own selected Legion hopefuls to attend.

"Commander Omar. What you're doing is borderline treason," a guard protests.

"Quit your bitching," Omar barks. "And if any of your worthless lot breathe a word of this, none of you will be breathing anymore."

Kasen and Vonnie hover there, beaten, baffled by Omar's sudden change. "Why?"

"Maybe some new blood around here isn't such a bad idea. But some advice before you start enjoying the finer things: If you're smarter than the average Slum, you won't mention your status. You'll participate in the exams tomorrow morning. And if you make me regret it, I'll immediately kill you and your little friend."

Kasen and Vonnie have achieved their first milestone. But there is still much work to do before life in the Slum is worth living—and neither have a clue where to begin.

COMPANIONSHIP

"**H**ey, Ashli! Wanna play tag?"
Kika attempts to wake her with a grin and a poke. Ashli herself had been in a meditative pose all night, and she's too concentrated to even answer.

"Fine. Then I'll find someone else to play with," Kika mopes, and stomps out the door.

Kika's sense of exploration (and her nose) take her to a small food court plaza within in the Commoner's District. There, workers are receiving a harsh yelling-at by their Higher Up boss.

"You Commoners convinced me that you were Evenrise's finest cooks, so why haven't I seen a single customer? Andre. Polina. Where are you?"

Two black and brown bear Bizarre navigate to the forefront of the group.

"You're in charge around here. You've boasted on and on about your culinary skills, but you failed to realize that no one cares anymore for barbaric meals."

"You're insulting not only fine cooks, but also war veterans." Polina speaks with the deep and burly Westerland accent, all its plush 'r's and chuffed 'v's. "We fought so you could have your riches in the first place, so the least you can do is be respectful."

"That's enough, Polina," Andre warns.

"Husband. You could break this man like a twig. How they've been treating us is unacceptable."

"I apologize for Polina," Andre tells the owner, but by the insult on the Higher Up's face, it's clearly not enough.

"I have no choice but to shut the plaza down, and have you deported to the Slum District. You'll have 'til the end of the day to gather your belongings." The owner waltzes away.

"Andre, what are we going to do?" sobs Polina. She supports her husband as he limps back to his seat at their steamed meats stand. A war injury—a spear through his leg—had never fully healed.

"Maybe he's right," Andre grumbles. "I was right to assume that once our old Ruler went off to train her daughter, new faces would take over and turn everything upside-down. It's just become too much."

As they grimly set about boxing their unbought meats, Andre and Polina hear the grunting of a young girl hopping to get a better look at a rotating brisket.

"You'll have to pay for that, little girl," Andre growls.

"Pay?" Kika repeats.

"Money, trade, or service. If not, skedaddle."

"What difference does it make now?" Polina cuts a small brisket piece for the girl. "Go on. At least someone's interested to try it."

The girl pops the brisket slice in her mouth in the same instant she's tossed it. Her eyes flare with delight.

"WOW! It's like playing tag with one person, then a lot more people come to play."

"That doesn't make sense," growls Andre. Polina can't help but laugh.

"No one's complimented our brisket like that. Eat as much as you like. Or at least within a few more hours."

Dancing in-place, smile threatening to devour her face, Kika snatches two fistfuls of meat and scrambles up the nearest building edifice to savor it.

"She's a strange one," Andre mumbles as Polina watches the little girl munching away overhead, swinging her legs as she feasts gleefully, without shyness or shame.

"Well, I think she's adorable," Polina notes.

"I'm not adorable," she protests, cheeks bulging. "I'm Kika."

Some faraway ruckus seems to have caught the girl's eye from her perch above the plaza. The next moment, she jumps down, the soles of her feet landing flat on the ground.

Polina hesitates only a moment. "Young lady, how'd you like a job?"

"We're not in a position to be offering jobs," Andre cuts in. "And no offense, young lady, but you don't seem reliable... at all."

"I like what we have and am going to work to keep it," snaps Polina. "Young lass. Those smug Higher Ups have made life difficult for the underprivileged. Many of us can't function like we used to. If you're willing to assist us in preserving the plaza, we'd sincerely be indebted to you."

"Hmm...bye!" Kika takes off, leaving Polina dumbfounded.

Andre sighs. "I'll start packing."

With their Exam invitation and guest passes in-hand, Kasen and Vonnie become the first Slum residents to cross through the Legion Academy doors.

Vonnie clutches on to Kasen tightly as they gaze around the inner academy. Its interior is held up by rows of stone pillars. Marble portraits of significant Apparitions make up the floor, and painted landscapes hang on every wall while crystal glass chandeliers hang from the ceilings.

At every turn, Apparitions wearing Legions academic uniforms are moving off to some unspecified business. If their formal blacks, blues, and violets weren't telling enough, the Legion insignia—the bold 'L' on the five-pointed star—is impossible to miss on every chest and arm.

Most of the students prove too occupied to notice two newcomers out-of-uniform—or that said newcomers are obviously not Higher Ups. Still, Omar's warning not to draw unnecessary attention to themselves burns at the back of Kasen's brain. Not wanting to push their luck, still tired from the morning's exertions, the newest recruits slip outside to rest in an unoccupied gazebo nestled between the grand academy corridors.

"Kasen, are you sure we can trust Omar?" Vonnie asks as they settle in. The scent of blooming flowers eases their anxiety, but only a little. "He probably wants to see us make fools of ourselves. Was leaving the District a good idea? Chantel was cruel, but she did take care of us."

Kasen doesn't want to give Vonnie a reason to doubt. He believed exiling Chantel was the right choice, but Vonnie wasn't wrong: it may make things worse for the Slum District. Not looking as he paces back and forth, he collides with a stranger, and falls over.

"Hiya," the stranger greets him with a wide grin—one you might call Devilish.

Minutes ago, Kika—having eaten her fill of brisket—found herself wandering onto academy grounds in search of a new friend to play with. Being friend to the Sacred Born had its perks. She could enter and leave the Academy as she pleased without guards harassing her.

She was drawn first to a group of gossiping girls around the fountain park. They were apparently in the middle of an important conversation.

"My dad told me they let outsiders into the city yesterday," one had just finished saying.

Another scrunched an eye. "Isn't that illegal or something?"

"Not when it comes to Edwin." One of her friends listening sighs when hearing his name.

"Now that's a real man. I told my parents to arrange a date, but they told me his busy schedule doesn't allow him to mingle. I doubt they even tried. What's the point of having parents if they don't do what you tell them?"

"You hate your parents, too?" Kika invited herself to their conversation. The well-off girls shot her snobbish stares.

"Who the hell are you?"

"Kika. Companion-seeker, seeking a companion. All one word."

"Ugh. They'll let anyone on campus now. Let's get out of here before she starts thinking *we're* her companions." The three girls laughed away, leaving Kika alone at the fountain.

"Bye!" Kika waved. "They seemed nice enough, but I don't need that many companions."

Kika continued her efforts on lakeside, where a handsome boy sat on a resting bench alone, vigorously rubbing a fragrance over his neck. Hearing sniffing sounds, he looked behind him to see Kika invading his personal space.

"Can I help you?" He scooted himself away from her. She didn't take the hint, and kept at her sniffing.

"You smell odd."

"Oh. It's the newest fragrance. My friends told me it's really good for getting lai—er. Smelling nice. Have a whiff." He sprayed it directly in Kika's face and she gagged.

"I meant 'bad' odd." She covered her nose.

"Surely you jest. This fragrance's one hundred percent guaranteed. I'd say *you're* the odd one. Besides, why should I care what you think, when I already have a..."

"There you are!" One of the girls from the fountain stormed over. "This is the third time this week I've seen you chatting up another girl. And—*ew*." She threw Kika the same snobby look. "My friends were so right about you. Enjoy your dumb tramp, you asshole."

She stomped off, tearful, sending the boy pleadingly chasing after.

"Guess he already had a companion," Kika figured. "This is harder than I thought. That one boy I saw earlier made it look so easy. Why don't I just ask how he does it? Then I'll have a companion in no time. Now, where'd he go?"

Dropping to all fours, Kika began sniffing the ground around her, renewed with purpose. Her behavior caught the attention of a crude old Legion soldier.

"Watcha doing down there, hun? looking for treasure?" He sidled closer to Kika, who carried on with her hunt, seemingly unaware of his presence. "I've got some treasure in my pants. How about you dig it out?"

"*Found you!*" Kika sprang to her feet, nose full of the scent she'd been looking for. The back of her head crushed into the center of the leering Legionnaire's face. She left him there with several broken teeth and a bloodied nose, none the wiser, hurrying along after her goal.

It led her right to the gazebo—and to the only two kids in the place who didn't stink.

Kasen blinks up at a girl's toothy smile from the ground. Where their collision had tipped him over, she barely budged.

"Um. Hi," Kasen stammers as he returns to his feet, feeling like he'd just run into a wall.

"Sorry. He didn't mean to run into you." Vonnie apologizes for him. "Are you OK, Kasen?"

"Well, that's rude," the strange girl replies.

Kasen feels a bit confused, to say the least. "That I didn't mean to?"

"I was looking for you because I need to find a new companion," she tells them. "And not just any companion—the best companion ever. We'll go on adventures, play tag, then play even more tag. I saw you become companions with that armored guy. Will you help me, please?"

'She mistook my confrontation with Omar for... play?' Kasen wonders, disbelieving. But he's not given much leeway to think it over.

"Hey. What are you doing?" he shrieks as the girl begins sniffing circles around them.

"It's you! How'd I not notice from the start? You don't smell odd like the others—not at all. You're my new companions, I just know it."

"I'm not sure if that's how having a companion works," Kasen fumbles.

"Please? If you aren't my new companions, I'll die." The girl sucks in and holds a breath. After a few moments pass, her face becomes blue and pale.

"C'mon, Kasen!" Vonnie urges. Seeing the girl suffocating is too much.

"Alright, fine. I mean, I guess." Kasen sighs. The girl cheerfully claps in celebration of her acquisition.

"I'm Kika. What are your names, new companions?"

"Nice to meet you, Kika. I'm Vonnie."

"Kasen..."

"Let's celebrate." That said, Kika grabs Kasen's arm.

Vonnie follows after as their new companion takes them to the food plaza in the Commoners District. The workers there are busy packing their equipment.

"You're back," Andre grumbles.

"And with new companions." She introduces Kasen and Vonnie.

"I'm literally surprised." Andre bluntly replies.

"'It's a pleasure to meet you both' is what my husband meant to say," Polina amends.

Kasen and Vonnie stand open-mouthed, scarcely able to believe the bounty surrounding them. It's exactly what they've been looking for. *Food*—enough for everyone in the Slums.

"Just a bite?" Vonnie tugs at Kasen's arm.

"We can't," he regrets.

"But Kasen. We can't help them if we're starving, too."

"If we eat while the rest of the Slum District starves, we're no better than Chantel."

"What was that, young man?" Andre demands, brow quirked in suspicion. Kasen had forgotten for a moment that they are still outsiders.

"He said: *If we eat before the rest of the Slum District,*" Kika impersonates, pitching her voice up into ridiculousness, *"We're no better than whatever-her-name-is."*

"You're Slum children?" The bear couple share grim looks—which turn into smiles—which turn into laughter.

"How didn't we notice?" Without another word, Polina digs into a packed crate, emerging with a fistful of fresh garments. They're a little big for Kasen and Vonnie, but better than their grime-soaked clothes.

"I don't understand. You're happy that Vonnie and I are Slums?" Kasen asks.

"There was a time when many of us fought to remove Evenrise's social laws. If you haven't already noticed, it didn't turn out so well."

"So... you got your asses kicked?" Count on Kika to supply the bluntest possible conclusion.

"No better way to describe it," Polina agrees. "But if you two have come here from the Slum District, this proves that things in this city are getting worse. We won't tell a soul."

"We're grateful for your kindness. But it doesn't feel right to just take these."

"Ahem. Can you excuse Kasen and me for a sec?" Vonnie pulls Kasen aside. Her whisper is sharp and reproachful. "These people are trying to help us. Why aren't you letting them?"

"Because I..."

"If we don't get food to the Slum District, they'll die. If you don't want to 'Chantel' this. This is how we do it."

"That's the point. We're not doing anything the way she did." Kasen leads Vonnie, sour-faced and hesitant, back to the vendors' stand. "We'll accept your help," he tells them, "once we've earned it. That way we all get something from it."

"Maybe there is a way for us to help each other," Polina suggests. "These ridiculous laws have made Higher Ups too hesitant to go beyond their district. But if you take some samples of our goods to them, maybe it'll convince a few to be more open-minded."

Andre shakes his head. "That's too much to ask from kids we know little about."

"My husband." Polina caresses his cheek. "You were once a proud soldier of Legion. I won't let some two-bit asshole who's never experienced battle or hardship walk all over you for another second. These people need you, these kids need you, but most important: I need you to do this with me."

Andre nods, sighs, and relents. "Very well. If you want our help, you'll earn your keep like the rest of us."

"Why did I invest in those has-been Commoners?" The owner bickers with himself as he returns to shut the plaza down, hurrying to finish his tasks before late afternoon settles in. "If they'd just accept the way things work around here, they'd be well-off."

A group of Apparition youths accidentally bumps into him as they hurry down the road. "Watch where you're...going?"

The bumpers only add to the crowd of Higher Ups milling before him, waiting to be served at the food stands. He pushes his way through.

"Just in time! Take an apron." Polina throws one to the owner, who fumbles it.

"Where did all these people come from?" he shrieks.

"If you're here to close us down," Andre pleads, but his voice is full of triumph, "can it wait until after we've served our guests?"

Upon hearing the word 'close,' the swarm of Higher Ups break out in noises of protest.

"Look at yourselves! This isn't how we behave," the beleaguered owner shouts at the crowd.

"You should keep an open mind." Andre offers the owner a roast slice that he smacks away.

"I'd sooner wipe my ass with it. My decision's final. I'm not wasting another cent on you worthless Commoners."

Polina spits at the owner's feet. "Bastard man with a tiny prick. No wonder you always act like one."

"Maybe deporting you all is too generous. The chopping block seems a better fit."

Legion soldiers barge their way through the gathered bodies.

"Just in time, gentlemen. Arrest these Commoners immediately," the owner demands.

"By order of the Fairest of Evenrise, this area's now under Legion management. The plaza and those working in it are to remain in operation until otherwise decreed." The soldier hands the owner the scroll with a special stamping.

"This is absurd. The plaza's bankrupt. Why would the Fairest approve such an outrageous order?"

"You'll have to take that up with the Council, sir... Hey, that smells good." The soldier helps himself to a free sample before he and his fellows depart.

"This isn't over. Mark my words." With nothing else to threaten, the owner storms off.

"Who's the Fairest of Evenrise?" Kasen asks, handing off another tray of sliced sausage.

"Evenrise's top law official," Polina answers. "Andre once held a position on his council. Then new laws started passing without Andre's input. The next thing he knew, he was being discharged."

"Interesting to see him going out of his way for our sake at the last moment," Andre says with skeptisim.

Business resumes at the plaza for the remainder of the afternoon. As promised, Andre and Polina offer what they can to help Kasen and Vonnie. But the Slum District has been on edge since Chantel's departure, and already, it's a different place than the one they left behind.

Arguments rage between residents over whether or not exiling Chantel was necessary—or prudent. The widow of the late Sampson,

Shannon, and her children can only watch the tension rise, as fights amongst the residents break out regularly.

Evening creeps toward the time Chantel appointed Shannon to perform services for the Legion guards again. Even with Chantel gone, her only means of keeping her family alive is to remain submissive to them.

Shannon hugs her two children before leaving for the gate. This time, she's tucked a shiv into her sleeve.

"I've arrived at the hour you requested." She knocks on the gate. "I've refused your demands to have my children watch, and accept the consequences of my actions."

She hopes they'll take the bait, and readies to attack the first guard she sees. Instead, a small package falls next to her. Its contents contain a small number of necessities—enough to lower the tension in the district for a while.

"It's the best we can do for now." Kasen's voice slips through from the other side of the gate.

"We haven't forgotten you. We're not as good at this as Chantel, but we're doing the best we can," says Vonnie.

"Why are you guys talking to a gate?" a third young voice puzzles.

"Just knowing that someone from the other side cares is good enough," Shannon replies. "You should hurry back before the guards arrive."

One last, mysterious voice—this one deep and ursine. "You don't need to worry about them anymore..."

On the other side of the gate, as the widow returns to her children with a parcel of food, the two guards who were moments ago so keen on their victim's visit had found themselves tied and gagged in an abandoned shack in the alley. They watch helplessly as the hefty bear Bizarre who'd jumped them cleans a rusted butcher's knife.

"Better run along, kids," adds a second bear Bizarre, whose kindly smile is terribly at odds with the dank surroundings and the dull gleam of the tarnished blade. "We'll catch up with you later."

Needing no further guidance, the young trio departs—leaving the captives alone with their captors.

"Gentlemen." Andre takes the chair before them. "Do I call you *gentlemen*, or is *cowards* your preferred term?"

The guards wiggle and grunt. Andre removes a rag from the mouth of the first.

"Jealous old-timer," he spits. "That thing between your legs not functioning properly? I know a broad who'll get it working in no time."

"Actually, it works just fine." Polina takes Andre's knife and stabs it into the guard's leg. She muffles his screams with a gag. The sight of blood and squirming sets his comrade to panicking, as well.

"Can't take the same pain you dish out?" She pulls the knife out and holds it between his legs. "You won't be needing this anymore."

She's about to slice the member, but before she does, the other guard's panic grows to an annoying zenith.

"You'll get your turn!" Polina points the knife at him. "Be patient."

"Let's hear him." Andre pulls the rag from the second guard's mouth.

"I haven't laid a finger on her, I swear. We aren't Legion soldiers, sir," he cries.

"Idiot," the first guard huffs around his mouthful of cloth.

"Please don't chop mine off—I haven't even used it yet..."

"If you aren't Legion soldiers, then who are you?" asks Andre.

"You better have a good answer, or I chop his off and have you choke on it," Polina warns.

"We're hired informants for the Band of Rogues, a major Feral group plotting to seize the city."

"I don't believe you. Feral are leaderless and too scattered. They don't have the numbers to be even a minor group."

"That's the truth, sir, I swear. Just please keep that knife away from me!"

"Is what he saying true?" Andre ungags the first guard.

"You're a fucking dumbass, Ralphie. But yeah, it's no secret Legion's been pussyfooting around for quite some time. Open season on this city's been declared." The guard laughs.

"Who's leading them?" Polina snaps. "They're leaderless; they war for no purpose."

"What difference does it make? I'm just getting whatever action I can before they kill you all. It was Ralphie's big night to become a man until you and your cronies jumped us."

"What should we do, Andre?" Polina asks.

"There's nothing you can do, you stupid bi—" Polina sticks the knife into the man's head before he can finish his sentence.

"Hate to admit it, but he has a point. Legion won't listen to Commoners, and would just assume we're spreading rumors. If these idiots managed to infiltrate Legion, no doubt more are scouring the city. We'll have to inform our new acquaintances. Perhaps they'll find out more."

"There's the Andre I know and love. Now, what do we do about this other non-soldier...?"

"We really owe you, Kika," Vonnie says, grateful for her help in achieving another milestone for the Slum District. "None of this would've been possible without you."

"I guess having a companion isn't a bad thing, after all," Kasen seconds.

"Companion? Oh, that's right. We were having so much fun, I forgot to introduce you to my OTHER companion. C'mon." Taking Kasen's arm again, Kika leads her new playmates to the guest suites of Legion Academy.

"I'm almost positive you'll get along great," Kika says as she opens the suite door. "I'm back!"

Kasen immediately recognizes the girl meditating in the center of the room. Once her eyes meet his, she attacks with a clean, straight kick that sends him hurling into the wall.

"Again?" Kasen coughs, finding his breath snatched away for the third time today.

His attacker plants her foot on his chest. Drawing her sword, she aims it for his throat.

"Ashli! Don't! They're my new companions," Kika pleads.

"Um. Ms. Ashli, " Vonnie asks politely. „Can you please let him go?"

Ashli sighs in annoyance as she removes her foot from Kasen. She exits the suite without saying a word.

"That went well," Kika says as Kasen regains his breath.

He hauls himself back to his feet. "Are you sure?"

"Positive. So, what game should we play next, new companions?"

Kasen holds out his Placement Exam invitation. Kika groans at the sight of it.

"It's a long story," he says.

"Fine. I'll go," she declares, looking none too happy, and that's that. "But only because we companions stick together."

It's enough. With Kika's help secured, Kasen and Vonnie have only to sleep—and to wonder what challenges await them at tomorrow's Placement Exam.

PLACEMENT EXAM

Becoming a Legion soldier is no simple task. Every year—or on those special occasions in which a Noble sponsors private invitationals—a class of recruits undergoes a series of difficult challenges. Their performance determines which of the seven divisions they'll be enlisted under.

Kasen, Vonnie, and Kika stand amidst the throng of other recruits in the academy courtyard. Ashli had taken a spot away from the crowd. The hopefuls around them make never-ending boasts about how they'll ace today's exam and become Legion soldiers. Outsiders who intend to watch the performance must view it from the stands, where they wager on their fates, as Higher Ups often do.

Omar and the other top-ranking officials watch them distantly from their positions at the podium. Once he raises his hand, the area falls silent.

"Welcome to Legion Academy's invitational Placement Exam. The Academy thanks Lord Edwin for sponsoring today's exam." Edwin kindly waves to the crowd under the applause. Omar proceeds. "Before we begin, we'll take a moment to address a certain issue at hand. As most of you are aware, Evenrise has been without Ruler for nearly two decades. After several meetings between the Fairest Council, top Legion officials, and Evenrise's main investors, we've decided on a temporary Ruler to hold the seat until our True Ruler is ready to accept the title. May I present our new Steward of Evenrise and Lord Commander of Legion, Sir Vincent!"

A middle-aged man, covered head to toe by a long black coat, takes Omar's place at the podium. His hood conceals most of his face. Only part of his burn-scarred cheek, a short goatee, and a piercing eye can be seen.

"Thank you, Commander Omar, and good morning all the recruits and citizens of Evenrise. I can already sense the concerns you may have. I confess I'm not well-known; I've mainly overseen Legion's sub-divisions. I understand your wariness at seeing an unfamiliar face take the role of Steward and Lord Commander. I merely ask that you see me as neither, but rather as a proud citizen of Evenrise who only wishes to uphold our customs and traditions, and to protect its people with my life. I welcome you, recruits, and anxiously look forward to watching you demonstrate your skills to become full soldiers and academics of Legion Academy." The crowd applauds him.

'A steward? You're kidding,' thinks Ashli, unimpressed.

"Without further delay: Let the exams begin!"

At Vincent's leave, Legion soldiers force their way into the crowd of recruits. They randomly separate them into smaller groups, and lead each to different challenge areas around the campus.

Kasen is among those separated from his friends. He and a few dozen other recruits are taken to a small, dark room beneath the academy. At least, that's what the recruits seem to assume.

"Excuse me, coming through. Hey, watch where you're grabbing." A young man squeezes his way through. Normish—with traits resembling a bird of prey. His arms are wings; his feet are talons. His Legion uniform, although crumpled and chronically unironed, sports several badges of recognition, although one wouldn't think so, judging from his lazy appearance.

He yawns. "Welcome to Edwin's sponsored Placement Exam. How's everyone doing today?" Not a single recruit responds. "Alright, then. I'm Larson, or Lars. I hold a Second Command position here at Legion, and I guess I'm examining your performance today."

"You're a Second Command? As in, you're next-in-line to be a Commander?"

"Sure. Why not. Let's get started. My superiors said I was to test your valor, fortitude, and something else I forgot. All I thought was: *hell, no*. I've got other things to do today, so we're trying something slightly different."

A single door opens to an underground coliseum track that stretches nearly a half-mile long. Heavy stones levitate in the air, lifted by an electromagnetic Aura. Spectators have already filed the stands. Among them are Omar and Vincent.

"All you have to do is get to the other side of the track. Should be easy enough," Lars informs.

"That's it?" a recruit blurts. "What kind of a Second Command are you?"

"There was another thing." Lars ponders a moment. "Oh, right. Only the first place winner proceeds to the next challenge; the rest will fail the exam and be escorted off campus."

Hearing this, the recruits shove their way through the small door. Kasen, who'd been standing at the back of the crowd, already finds himself at a disadvantage.

The group Vonnie had been put with was ushered off to a shaded picnic area. They sit on laid-out blankets, where soldiers serve tea. Their examiner: a large sloth Bizarre wearing a tropical-themed uniform. (He never liked Legion standard colors, so he's customized his own.)

"Beautiful day for an exam, wouldn't you agree, recruits?" He delightfully sips his tea. "I can tell just by looking that most of you aren't suited for Legion." His comment unnerves several of the recruits seated around him. "Nevertheless, I'm a reasonable man, and am giving you an opportunity to prove me wrong. Anyone care to sit with me and have a pleasant chat?"

An eager recruit quickly takes initiative and accepts the offer.

"A pleasure making your acquaintance, young recruit. I'm Legion's Infiltration Division Commander, Sloth."

"Aren't you a bit big for—?"

"For what?" Sloth wonders.

"Never mind." And the recruit and Sloth begin to have a normal conversation.

As they chat, Vonnie worries. How will she talk with Sloth without revealing she's from the Slum District? *'I hope Kasen and Kika are doing alright...'*

DOM BRANDT

Kika and her group are taken to a small field. Before them sit two vast boulders and a single levitating cube.

They've the pleasure of having no-nonsense, short-tempered Jaquelin as their instructor. Jaq, as she demanded to be called, is a tall, tan, toned woman. Her tough posture alone is enough to frighten the recruits.

"Listen up, you little shits," she barks. "If you thought today was going to be a piece of cake, you can see your asses off campus right now. Only strength matters at Legion. Lift any one of these three objects, and I'll decide which division you'll be placed under. Now quit standing around like a bunch of idiots and get on with it."

"Just—just lift it?" a recruit stammers.

"Are you repeating what I just said?" Jaq growls.

"S—Sorry, ma'am." The recruit tries lifting the levitating cube and promptly throws out their back in the process.

"The cube's obviously the heaviest, you dumbass. Get the hell outta here, and never show your face on campus again."

The recruit cries as they run off.

Kika, meanwhile, has gotten herself lost in her own world as the other recruits tremble fearfully around her. *'Wonder how Ashli's doing…?'*

"This is pointless."

Ashli and several other recruits stand aligned upon a balance board that stretches over a small pond. Aura properties make it spin at nauseating paces. Recruits with poor balance and those quick to dizzy find themselves splashing into the water. Soon, only Ashli and one other recruit, clinging the board for dear life, remain.

"You gotta help me, lady," her struggling competitor begs, scraping for a better grip on the beam. "My family's super rich and we have our fingers in some deep pockets. Take the fall, and I promise you'll have enough to never work a day for the rest of your life."

Ashli replies by stepping on their hand. Surrendering to the pain, they let go, and splash into the pond.

"You've considerable talent, young lady," the examiner compliments. "Proceed down the path for the next challenge."

'Why would Mother ever want to become a Ruler of these obnoxious fools?'

Ashli wonders. Her thought's interrupted by Edwin's clapping. He is the only spectator in the area.

Kasen has finally gotten through the door. Upon reaching the track, he breaks into a run, lagging behind the rest of the recruits.

"Enjoy failing, losers!" jeers the recruit in first place, who'd gained a solid gap ahead of the competition.

A few of the floating rocks fall within inches of Kasen. His heartbeat skyrockets from the near-death experience.

At seeing a fellow runner nearly crushed, many recruits abandon their efforts to continue as floating rocks descend onto the track. Others scatter and scurry off-course, disqualifying themselves. Kasen, on the other hand, weaves his way through the mayhem until the finish line stands less than one hundred yards away.

As the rocks pile higher, threatening to make crossing impossible, Kasen sprints faster, and—just before the last rock blocks the finish—he dives over the remaining gap.

The spectators in the stands murmur to another. None seem to know the contender who has claimed victory.

Lars comes to congratulate the exhausted Kasen at the finish. "Nicely done, Mister...kid? Huh. Well, alright. Let's get you off to the next challenge."

"You're a riot." Sloth has been laughing since the start of his one-on-one conversation.

"So since we've been getting along pretty good, how about making me a Legion Soldier?"

"Oh, I'm sorry, but I'm afraid I can't do that," Sloth calmly informs his current interviewee.

"What? Why not?" the recruit shrieks. "Honestly, when weren't you laughing? I come from a family of Legion soldiers; I'm not going to be the one who ends the chain."

"There's nothing wrong with family tradition. There's also nothing wrong with going a different path, either."

The recruit kicks over Sloth's tea kettle assortment. "You'll make me into a Legion soldier or my family will have you deported to the Slum District, you tea-loving freak."

Sloth deeply sighs. "That assortment belonged to my dearly departed Gram."

He hits the recruit with a quick jab, and they crumple to the ground, whining like a child.

"Please escort this recruit off campus." Legion guards haul them off.

"So, who'd like to be next?" Sloth looks through the waiting recruits. His eyes land on Vonnie. He gestures for her to sit beside him.

Butterflies fill her stomach, her arms riddled with goosebumps. Vonnie looks at the ground to avoid the stares of the other recruits as she walks over to Sloth. He smiles warmly. She tries imitating the expression, but can't get her smile past *meek*. Sloth offers her tea.

"Th—thanks." She takes a nervous sip, tasting sweetness on her lips.

"*I'm sure that after seeing what happened to the last recruit, you're feeling less confident, but you have no reason to be shy, young lady. All I'm going to do is ask you one question, and I need you to listen as closely and carefully as you can. You're a resident of the district beyond the gates, aren't you?*" Sloth had spoken to her telepathically. "*You have my word: none can hear us so long as we speak like this. Concentrate your thoughts, and I will hear them.*"

"*Er...like this?*" Vonnie projects back.

"*As I gazed at the recruits, I read their minds, and why they chose to become Legion soldiers. And, as always, most are here for the wrong reasons. Forgive me for prying into your thoughts. But what you were thinking was passionate and sincere. I wish to aid your efforts, and would be honored to have you in my division.*"

"Pathetic! All of you!" Jaq shrieks, watching another recruit fail to lift a rock. She sees Kika hasn't yet tried. "Little girl, have you been standing around this whole time?"

"Who, me?" Kika looks around.

"Who else?"

"Oh. What are we doing?"

Jaq is obviously reaching her boiling point. "Use your flimsy little hands and lift one of those rocks."

Kika happily complies. Bounding over to the lightest boulder, using both hands, she manages to lift it up and over her head.

"Well, at least someone has some potential," Jaq grumbles. "I suppose you'd make a decent patrol officer."

"Wanna play a game?" Kika asks.

Jaq's mouth drops when she shifts the bolder to one hand and lifts the heavier boulder with the other. With her teeth, she clamps the levitating cube, spits it onto her foot, and juggles it from one leg to the other.

"Uh. Er. Just go that way." Jaq points out the path leading to the next challenge.

"OK. Goodbye, new friend." Kika drops her toys. The earth shakes when they hit, and she continues happily down the path.

"Who the hell was that?" Jaq wonders, speechless.

"Hi, companion!" Kika greets Kasen when they reunite. They join the few others who also completed the first challenge. Although Kasen feels relieved to see a familiar face, it worries him that Vonnie isn't present.

"And hello, super pal," Kika welcomes Ashli as she strides up to stand beside her. Vincent, Omar, and Lars arrive moments later.

"Congratulations on completing your first challenge, recruits," Vincent commends. "Our sponsor has demanded that we wrap this exam up, so this next challenge is all-or-nothing."

Lars walks around giving the recruits slips of paper. Each of them contains a math equation.

Kasen's reads: 21/3

Ashli's: (126x11/18)/11

And Kika's: -6+13

"What are these supposed to be?" The recruits study their slips.

"Pretty simple. If the answer to the equation equals seven, you've been recruited into Legion's Elite Division. If not, go home."

Bickering commences amongst the recruits. Only three managed to pass.

"I passed? Son-of-a-bitch." Kika rips her slip.

"Are you kidding?" a recruit complains. "I've trained for years to become a Legion soldier and I'm outdone by a piece of frickin' paper?"

"No exceptions," Omar barks.

The recruits who failed grumble as Legion guards escort them off Academy grounds. Kasen sighs with relief, and a feeling of accomplishment washes over him.

"This is ridiculous," Ashli snarls.

Lars seems mildly surprised. "Only three?"

"Three more than I assumed," Omar growls.

"It seems Edwin's boasting about you wasn't just talk, Sacred Born," says Vincent. "And the Sacred Born's bubbly friend that he mentioned. I'm interested to see what you have to offer, as well."

"Yeah. Neat," Kika mumbles.

Vincent turns to Kasen. "I can't say I'm familiar with you, young man."

"He won that race you designed yourself, Lord Commander," Lars reports.

"Ah, yes—that last-second stunt. I suppose I'll be looking forward to all three of you."

"It'll take more than a few stunts to impress me," Omar disagrees. His hard gaze settles on Kasen. "Show them the ropes, Second Command."

Having congratulated all they cared to, Omar and Vincent depart.

"OK, then. Who's ready for a field trip? If not, too bad. Welcome to your first day as Legion soldiers, kiddos."

ELITES-IN-TRAINING

"**O**nly three?!" barks Jaq as Lars and the newly-accepted soldiers meet her squadron at the main gates of Evenrise.

"Good morning to you, too, Jaquelin."

"Don't call me—! Never mind. We've got scouting work to do." She narrows her tough gaze on the newcomers. "Don't think for a second that because you're Legion soldiers, you're not still at the bottom of the pecking order. We're your superiors, and you'll obey our orders without question. Got it? You'd better."

'*Who does this woman think she is?*' Ashli thinks, rolling her eyes.

"We're really going outside of Evenrise?" Kasen asks.

"That a problem? Or did you have somewhere to be with your boyfriend?"

"Er...no?"

"Ha. I knew it," says Kika.

The main gates open on Lars's command, revealing the flat and dry land surround the perimeter of the civilization.

The Southerlands—or everything south Evenrise—was mostly made up of vast fields. Beyond these fields lay the tropical forest, and beyond that, the open sea. The Uncharted Territories took most of the general Northerland, and far in the Westerland stretched the Ancient Desert. Evenrise itself was nestled in the eastern hemisphere.

As the Legion soldiers travel the north roads, Kasen marvels. Never in a million years had he thought he'd see the lands beyond Evenrise. He wishes Vonnie were here beside him to witness it, as well.

"So, companion. Want to play hide-n'-seek?" asks Kika.

"How?" Kasen looks around. There aren't many hiding spots on an open plain.

"Simple. You go hide, I'll count to a random number, and come look for you."

"I meant how can we, when there isn't..."

"Whoever you are." Ashli coldly interrupts Kasen. "I don't know or care how you managed to get this far, but if you even so much as slightly get in my way, or put Kika in any danger, I swear not to leave a trace of you." Her threat chills Kasen to the bone.

"Something tells me you two will get along just fine." Kika pats Kasen on the back.

"So, Jaq," Lars digs as their subordinates whisper. "You still upset at losing to me for the Second Command position?"

"Our orders are to investigate the old storage facility," she cuts back, ignoring him.

"I thought Legion had a team take care of it already?"

"These aren't the brain-dead Feral we've usually dealt with. They're well-armed and manned. They anticipated an attack. The Legion soldiers didn't stand a chance."

"Then let's take care of them ourselves. This Feral situation's been getting out of hand for months now."

"You're on babysitting duty, Second Commander." Jaq peers back at the three, and judging by the bland shadow that crosses her face, she clearly doesn't see much of a future for them at Legion.

They journey a few short miles across the fields, approaching an abandoned warehouse hidden between a small cluster of healthy pines. Jaq orders the group to keep low and remain quiet. Peering from behind the trees, they watch slave-drivers forcing their captives to haul and stack large crates. A menacing drawn Black Hand emblem gleams on each one.

The Feral leader stands in the scant shade of the warehouse, talking business with their new partners. They're unmistakable to Kasen, even at this distance: Juan and Yuan.

"So, what are you guys, anyways?" The Feral leader asks. Juan and Yuan blink back at him, holding hands.

"We're business professionals," Juan answers.

"What else could we be?" adds Yuan, but doesn't let go of Juan's hand.

'Well, good for them for making strides, at least,' Kasen thinks to himself, and sighs. There's no use even wondering how they've gotten themselves involved in this mess yet. As the group retreats back inside, he puts on his best blank look to ask: "Who are they?"

"Feral," replies Lars. "The name says it all. "They're a violent type who normally dwell in the deep forest and mountains. They've become more of a nuisance since they began establishing camps within a short distance of the city."

"Scout the interior. Get an estimate on hostiles and hostages," Jaq orders her men.

Kasen watches as an elderly slave falls from exhaustion. The crate he'd carried cracks open and leaks a thick black liquid. Some of it splatters on the shoe of a slave driver. The elder quickly prostrates himself before his master and begs to be forgiven. Instead, the slave-driver kicks him several times over. The other slaves continue to work in fear of receiving the same punishment.

"This asshole got his blood all over my shoe." The other slave-drivers laugh.

"Damn those bastards," Lars snarls. His face boils as his fist clenches.

"Don't even think about it, Second Command," Jaq warns Lars. "It's hard to watch, but we don't have clearance or the numbers to storm them."

"Screw the damn clearance. I'll take care of them myself!"

As Lars readies himself, the black sword appears in Kasen's hand. It tugs him along against his will, and he follows, dragged along as if by some form of possession.

"What the hell do you think you're doing?" Jaq shrieks.

"Playing hide-n'-seek, duh." Kika begins counting.

Kasen tries resisting whatever has taken hold of him, but his efforts are futile. The unknown force clamping down on him settles after a few moments, but not before bringing him in clear view of the Feral.

"That idiot," Jaq spits.

"Who the hell are you?" A Feral approaches him, and their attention draws to black sword in his hand. "That's a nice-looking toy. How many of your limbs do I need to break for you to hand it over?"

Kasen hesitates. "What you're doing to these people is wrong," he says, finally, mustering his courage.

DOM BRANDT

"Then do something about it, tough guy."

Before he can even dream about it, a figure sweeps past the Feral, leaving a deep slash across their waist. Kasen grimaces with disgust as the insides pour out. He feels as though he might vomit.

It is Ashli who cut down the Feral; she proceeds quickly to her next target.

"Found you, Companion." Kika runs to Kasen. "You suck at hide-n'-seek."

"Guess it doesn't matter anymore." Lars pats an angered Jaq before rushing in to help eliminate the remaining Feral.

"Another empty victory," Ashli mulls after the perimeter of the warehouse is secured.

"You kids took the spotlight right out from under me," Lars says as he pulls his sword from a Feral.

"So. You're not pissed?" Kika asks.

Kasen tries explaining himself. "I don't know what happened, or how it happened, I swear. I—"

"We'll worry about that later. Let's clear the hostages and see what's going on inside the warehouse," says Lars.

"Second Commander Larson." Jaq and her men stand ready for confrontation nearby. "Defying the orders of a superior officer's a serious offense. Don't think this behavior won't go unpunished."

"This place should've been cleared out months ago, Jaq," Lars counters. "We can clear out these Feral ourselves."

"I knew your ego would get out of hand. Stand down, or consider yourselves traitors." Her loyalists draw weapons.

"You don't frighten me." Ashli looks prepared for battle—but Lars steps in front of her.

"There's a reason I bested you for the Second Command position. And with your head so far up your ass, you keep forgetting who's really in command. So, as your commanding officer, I command you and your men to stand down and escort the labors to a secure location, while the the trainees and myself deal with any remaining hostiles."

"Second Command…" Jaq gives Lars one final cold glare before she and her men sheath their weapons. "…for now."

Nevertheless, they begin to escort the hostages to safety.

"She seems nice," Kika says.

"She's alright. Rumor's that she just got out of a really bad relationship, and with not qualifying for Second Command position at the same time, I'd probably be a constant asshole to everyone, too... but probably not."

Lars kicks open the doors of the warehouse. The few rays penetrating the holes in the walls and ceiling offer some visibility. Rusted pipes and rails run along its walls and three level balconies. A round pool in the center contains the same black liquid the slaves have been hauling.

"That doesn't look welcoming. Stick close, kiddos," Lars says.

"Isn't that the fun of adventure?" Kika goes over to the pool, makes to scoop a handful.

"I wouldn't do that, little girl," warns a woman standing on the highest balcony, two identical young men at her sides. And the group finds itself surrounded by Feral.

"Chantel!" Kasen shrieks.

"You again?" Juan and Yuan shriek back.

"Are they companions of yours?" asks Kika.

"Not even close."

"Chantel? Where have I heard that name?" Lars's expression turns searching as he hunts down the memory. "No way," he dismisses when it dawns on him. "It can't be THAT Chantel."

"I see you've made some new friends, little thief. Or is it that you've found more lives to ruin?" Juan and Yuan snicker at her barb.

"What are you scheming now, Chantel?"

"After you had me shunned from the Slum District, I had to go back to my full-time job. The black liquid you see before you is a manufactured Aura still in development. We're having trouble harnessing it. Observe."

At the snap of her fingers, the Feral gang up on who they believe to be the weakest among them, and toss them into the black pool. It bubbles as if boiling, and a horrid reptilian creature emerges from its depths. It thrashes about it the pool, attacking anything in reach of its razor-sharp teeth and claws. The Feral step away, but one doesn't step far enough, and the creature chomps down and gruesomely devours them. Then it suddenly petrifies, and crumbles to nothing.

"What the hell just happened?" Lars gasps.

"Not the best result," Chantel notes, "but it's good for making standard weapons. Which is also fine."

Kasen's body runs cold as the surface of the substance stills. "What do you plan to do with them?"

"Good question, little thief. I'd like to open up my own petting zoo, but there's also the option of waging war on Evenrise."

"Tough choice," Kika adds.

"All you are is another simple-minded Feral," says Ashli. "I'll drive my blade through you, and your pitiful ambitions."

"No. We need to retreat now!" Lars shrieks, frightened. "We need to notify the superiors. Evacuate Evenrise, before she destroys everything."

"I won't let that happen," Kasen swears. "I learned the hard way what happens when you just idly stand by. If she's been stopped before, she can and will be again. Besides, Chantel knows she can't accomplish her plans without this."

With a gesture of great defiance, Kasen holds out his hand for the black sword.

Nothing appears.

"Oh, cool, an arm. Wish I had one," Kika says.

Kasen blinks at his empty hand, dumbfounded.

"Well, I've had enough shenanigans for today. You can kill them now."

The Feral go after Kasen. Ashli spares him from a cruel fate, slaying each attacker herself.

"You're completely useless," she snarls at Kasen, and ascends to the third balcony to face off against Chantel.

Kika tries cheering Kasen up. "It's OK, companion."

"She's right," he mopes. "I am useless."

"Um…duh?"

Above the Aura pit, Chantel watches Ashli gain ground, and turns to her servants. "Juan, Yuan. I'll reconvene with you once I've finished here. This one appears to be a tad stronger than the others."

"Either way, show her no mercy, my lady." Juan and Yuan make their escape through a hole in the wall.

"After you're finished here?" Ashli dares, hauling herself the last few feet onto the balcony. "Are you that arrogant?"

"I know that look all too well. You definitely take after Kiera, Sacred Born. Unlike her, I have no desire of making you my enemy."

"Anyone acquainted with that vile woman's my enemy." Ashli attacks. Despite her speed and ferocity, Chantel catches her wrist mid-attack.

"Here's some advice to go home with. Compared to me, Sacred Aura is hardly even a joke." Chantel breaks Ashli's wrist just by squeezing with her hand, then she punctures into her abdomen. Ashli jumps back. Her broken arm goes limps to her side, and she clutches her wound with her able arm. Grunts of pain escape her.

"Your mother must've never informed you, Sacred Born, but there ARE powers in this world that dwarf Sacred Aura. Kind of makes me wonder how well you truly know Kiera. If you hunger to go well beyond what you are, I'd be more than happy to show you the way."

'Who is this woman?' Ashli wonders, shocked, enfeebled by her wound. 'No such power exists...'

"Hunger? There's food up there?" Kika is already climbing up the pipes. "Quit hogging it, Ashli."

Chantel raises a single finger. A small black light illuminates from its tip.

"Just a tease of what this power can do." Chantel flicks the black light in Kika's direction, and it darts towards her.

"Kika! Move out of the way!" Ashli shouts through her pain. Before the black light connects with its intended target, Kasen jumps in the way of the black flicker. A sharp pain runs through him as it digs into his chest. Everyone gasps.

"Goodbye, little thief," Chantel says only. The black flicker inside Kasen detonates, leaving a gaping hole in the center of his chest. The force of it launches him into over and into the black liquid pool.

"No! No! No!" Lars frantically crawls over beside the pool. Ashli musters the composure to leap down to him and Kika.

"I know you're hiding in there, companion. You can come out now," Kika shouts.

"Kika." Ashli shakes her head.

"But...he's my companion," she whimpers.

"I'm Second Command of Elite Division. How could I let this happen?" Lars sobs.

"He died as pathetically as he lived." Chantel drops down to the remaining three. "So. Who's next?"

The black liquid begins boiling more furiously than before. Rising from its circular confinement, changing from its black color to a dark green. It funnels into the black sword now held in Kasen's hand. Kasen himself levitates in the center, unconscious, but the wound in his chest has been completely healed.

"Kid?" Lars marvels.

"Companion?" Kika asks.

"Little *thief*...."

Hearing Chantel's voice, a burst of Aura propels Kasen at her. His incoming attack catches her by surprise, and the next thing Chantel knows is that she's being launched into the ceiling. And crashing onto the third balcony.

"Again. What the hell is going on?" Lars, astonished, demands.

"What the hell IS going on?" Ashli agrees.

"Well. Wasn't expecting that." Chantel gets to her feet—but has little time to process what happened before Kasen continues his assault against her. She soon realizes how much Kasen has dramatically changed.

"Idiot little thief! I told you that you had no idea about the sword, and now it's possessing you." Chantel leaps to a hole in the wall. "Let me know when you decide to take this more seriously." So saying, she makes her escape.

With Chantel gone and no more enemies remaining, the black sword disappears. Kasen's caught by Lars as he falls to the ground level.

"He's alive," Lars sighs. "We need to take him to the infirmary."

They exit the warehouse. Awaiting them outside is the entire Elite Division, with weapons drawn.

"I said you wouldn't go unpunished," Jaq thunders.

"Sheesh. About time you woke up, kid," is the first thing Kasen hears as he groggily awakens.

The area is dark, dank. The air holds a thin stench. The sounds of water echo around him. It's murky, and drip-drops echo down the walls of these dark chambers.

"What happened? Where are we?" Kasen looks around. A prison—that much he can tell.

"The Academy holding cells." Lars lies across a rusted old bench. "These haven't been used in while, since now they just deport everyone to the Slum District. You've been out a few days now, kid."

"A few days?" Kasen shrieks.

"Yeah, that's definitely not good."

Footsteps on the hard floors beyond their cell alert them. Then, a voice: *"As you wish, Commander Sloth."*

A guard opens a door, allowing Vonnie, Ashli, and Kika in. A sloth Bizarre in officer attire accompanies them.

"Vonnie!" Kasen blurts, relief washing over him. "Your clothes?"

She, too, was wearing the Legion uniform. For now, she does not explain. "You look terrible," she tells him.

"Companion, I knew you wouldn't die," says Kika.

"Kika? Ashli? Why aren't you two in cells?"

"They've been pardoned," Commander Sloth informs him. "I guess someone of high influence didn't want the Sacred Born imprisoned."

"Alright. Now that the gang's all here, you have some explaining to do, kid."

So Kasen and Vonnie tell everyone the whole story. Their lives in the Slum District, Chantel, and the fight to end the social laws of Evenrise.

"With Chantel active again, it means Evenrise is in deep," Lars murmurs.

Sloth, for his part, commends Kasen. "You're considerably more courageous than Vonnie described."

"I'm sorry. I never planned to get you all involved," he regrets.

Lars shrugs. "Well, in a way, you saved my ass, so we're good."

"For now, at least." Omar growls as he enters the cells. The soldiers salute without hesitation as their Commander's menacing gaze immediately redirects itself to lock upon Kasen. "I gave you one simple instruction, Slum boy. How did you even survive in that district with stupidity like yours?"

"Wait. Commander Omar. You knew?" asks Lars.

"It's not your concern, Second Command. I had to pull a lot of strings to have you both stand before the Fairest Council, so you better not embarrass my Division again. I've no patience for wannabe heroes and egocentric morons. Am I understood?"

"Yes, Commander." Lars's voice trembles.

"S—Sorry," Kasen peeps.

"Tsk. Fucking morons." Omar is about to leave—until Sloth steps in his way.

"Commander Omar. You've no reason to speak harshly to your subordinates. They may have disobeyed orders, but it was only to protect this city. If you have knowledge of the threat that looms over us, then things do need to change, and quickly."

"You've grown soft, Infiltration Commander. Soft, and fat, and if you don't move aside, I'll show you just how soft and fat."

It's a short standoff. Omar's position as Elite Division Commander is all he needs for an Infiltration Commander to stand down, and he shoulder checks Sloth to remind him of that.

"Yeah. Well, at least we weren't bottle-fed." Kika sticks out her tongue at Omar's back as he storms away.

"I think that's enough drama for today." Lars yawns.

"I agree," says Sloth. "You boys will need your rest if you're going up against the Council."

"Be strong, Kasen," Vonnie tells him. "Are you coming, Kika?"

"Hm. I don't think you would two make a good pair." Kika glances between Kasen and Lars. "Bye, companion."

Ashli remains after everyone else leaves.

"I know when I'm a third wheel." Lars plops back on the bench.

"Why you were willing to sacrifice yourself for Kika?" she asks.

"Because I meant it when I said I wouldn't let Chantel hurt anyone. Kika saved a lot of people the other day. I couldn't be more grateful to her. She's a good friend, and again, I'm sorry I got you involved in this. I need to stop apologizing all the time," Kasen rambles, losing the thread of of his speech.

'Since when does having friends give you newfound powers? That Chantel woman. Whoever she was. Was she telling the truth when she talked about powers greater than Sacred Aura?' Ashli wonders.

"Something wrong?" Kasen asks, seeing her lost in thought.

"Worry for your own wellbeing. If what you said is true, then get out of this mess you've made. Then perhaps you won't be completely useless."

"OK?" Kasen wasn't sure if that Ashli was complimenting or insulting him.

"And that obnoxious Chantel woman—she will be destroyed."

THE FAIREST OF EVENRISE

Kasen and Lars awaken to cold water splashing over them. Guards had entered their cell, and place them in shackles.

"Get moving," one barks, and they do.

They are taken through the underground corridors of the Academy, proceeding up a few flights of stairs and coming to a white door that a guard opens. Kasen squints under the bright morning sun from the window of Legion's grand courtroom. Rows of pews are filled with murmuring Higher Ups and Legion officials. Five judge seats in front oversee all.

Kasen and Lars are placed in the defendant seats facing the pews. They have the pleasure, Kasen notices, of sitting right in front of Ashli and Kika.

"Hey, companion," Kika casually hellos. "What's with the chains? Are you trying to live out a fantasy?"

"Don't be absurd," Ashli snaps.

"Let's try keeping a cool head, everyone. Just let me do the talking," Lars instructs, "and hopefully our punishment will be community service."

"You could've picked a better spot," Vonnie complains to Commander Sloth in the meantime from their position in the middle back pews. She's too small to see over the taller Apparitions.

"I can see just fine," Sloth chuckles.

"Kasen should know at least someone here is supporting him."

"Do you really want to see him in this condition?"

"Of course I don't," Vonnie replies. "He didn't do anything wrong."

"I'm assuming Second Command Lars has thought of a way to win over the Council. All we can do is hope for the best."

FOREVER WILL END

"Ladies and Gentlemen. Direct your attention forward," an announcer shouts, and the murmuring falls silent. "All members of the Fairest Council will preside over today's hearing. First to take his seat, Vice Lord of Legion Academy, and its Commander of Elite Division, Sir Omar."

Omar appears, decked in his usual full armor, and takes the far right seat.

"Recently elected member of the Fairest Council, Sir Trexler."

A short brown- and black-scaled reptilian Bizarre takes the far left seat, dressed in a noble suit with Legion insignia embedded on the left breast and upper back. He bickers grumpily with himself.

"Steward of Evenrise and Lord Commander of Legion, Sir Vincent."

The Lord Commander takes the inside seat next to Omar, most of his face still hidden under a hood.

"Commander of Legion's Medical Division and Senior Adviser, Lady France."

An elderly gray and black feline Bizarre takes her seat next to Trexler. France had been with the Fairest Council for a few decades, and in her archaic green and maroon dress, appears less irritated than the other three.

Everyone in the courtroom rises to their feet. Lars has to prompt Kasen, Ashli, and Kika to do the same as an old mink Bizarre, leaning on a cane, makes his way to the center seat.

"All rise for the Fairest of Evenrise, one of Evenrise's very own original founders and widely regarded as the wisest Apparition of the known land. We're honored to have Fairest Gyra preside over today's hearing."

Though no one knew for sure, Gyra was estimated to be in the eighty-to-ninety rage. If not hunched over, he'd have been around Omar's height. Beneath the black judge's robes and platinum chest plate, his brown fur was clearly drying out, leaving gray and balding patches; his long, braided beard hung low from his chin and, today, his eyes are barely open.

"That's the big cheese," Lars whispers to Kasen. "Gyra's sole duty is to make sure all citizens obey the laws of Evenrise to the letter. We'll choose our words carefully with him."

"Be seated," Gyra orders. Everyone is quick to obey. "This trial is now in session. Second Command of Elite Division Lars and a new recruit of the Elite Division, Kasen, both stand accused criminal negligence and insubordination. It's not everyday we see ranking officials convicted of these crimes, but your intentionally putting your own squad in danger has made us question how much you're willing to risk."

"Why bother having a trial?" Trexler shrills. "Criminals don't deserve the right to explain their actions."

"Patience, Trexler," France calms him. "They've been given the opportunity, regardless of what you believe."

"I'm rather intrigued by this." Vincent caresses his beard. "To storm a Feral camp and emerge unscathed requires great cunning."

"I still think they're idiots," Omar growls.

"Plain and simple, I'm disappointed." Gyra's conclusions come harsh and quick. "I expect Legion's high-ranking officials to serve as positive role models for our younger generation, and their trainees aren't permitted to act irresponsibly, either."

"With all due respect, Your Fairest." Lars stands up. "The fault lies with me. My trainee was—"

"I've done this for many years, Second Command. "Don't think for a second I'll be swayed by honeyed words and charming gestures. If you're both convicted, you shall be punished appropriately, are we clear?"

"Of course, Your Fairest." Lars plops back into his seat.

"We'll start with the primary witness. To the stand: Miss Jaquelin."

Lars groaned, clearly assuming Jaq would take any opportunity to relieve his position as Second Command. "Here we go."

"Thank you, Your Fairest." Jaq lightly bows. "I'll explain exactly how I remember it. A few days ago, our team was tasked to observe Feral activity at the north warehouse. The Feral there had turned it into a labor camp to make weapons, as we had suspected. I'm sure Lars intends to convince you all fault lies with him. The truth is that he's only doing so in fear for his life. The true fault lies with the trainee, Kasen."

Kasen feels thousands of volts shoot through him at the mention of his name. The murmurs among the crowd are revived.

"He drew his sword on us, even though he was order not to act," she continues. "He wanted to make a name for himself. He threatened that if we got in his way, he'd kill us, and say we were enemies of Evenrise." Jaq wipes away a fake tear. "After he compromised our position, it was

Lars's swift action that allowed me to testify before you today. I kept this from the pulic because the trainee swore that if we told anyone, he'd come after our families."

Gasps fill the room. Kasen suspects the Higher Ups don't care about what's true or not—so long as there is someone to blame.

"The fiend," Trexler shrieks.

"Sheesh, what a bitch," Kika whispers to Ashli, who remains quiet.

"That's the truth, Your Fairest, and members of his Council. On my position, I swear it to you." Jaq wipes her eyes again.

"Thank you for sharing. We know speaking the truth can be difficult in times of stress," France says.

"I just want justice. Behavior like his doesn't save people; it gets them killed."

"Be seated, Miss Jaquelin." Gyra thanks her. She bows once more. As she returns to her seat, Lars gets her attention.

"What the hell was that?" he sharply whispers at her.

"I'm getting your ass out of your mess—like Omar wanted," she sharply whispers back. "Your trainee's a nobody. Who cares what happens to him?"

"That's enough bickering, you two." Gyra cuts them off. "To the stand, trainee," he orders Kasen.

Kasen thinks—and hopes—he'll die from the anxiety. Slowly, yet surely, he rises from his seat to stand before the Council.

"Have you anything to say in your defense against the accusations made against you?"

"I—I—" Kasen can't find his words.

"That the only word you know? Speak up, boy," Omar barks.

"I didn't," Kasen blurts. *'You don't have any room to talk, Omar,'* is what he wants to say.

"You'll have to be more convincing than that, young man," France warns him.

"I'm sorry. I don't remember much." Kasen's replies only elicit more murmuring from the Higher Ups in the pews.

"He's stalling," Trexler snaps.

"How's a new recruit able to hold his superior hostage?" Vincent asks.

"Memory loss doesn't excuse your crimes," Gyra adds.

"I remember after storming the base," Kasen offers, but is cut off.

"Are you admitting your crimes?" Trexler dares.

"There's more." Kasen speaks clearly now. "The Feral were under the command of Chantel. She's plotting to attack Evenrise." Where others failed, it is this claim that inspires the Fairest Council to exchange looks with each other.

"Chantel, you say?" Gyra postulates.

"It's true, Your Fairest," Lars agrees. "I didn't believe it at first, either, but she's definitely up to something sinister."

"I can't image how a young lad like yourself has knowledge of Chantel. She was confirmed dead in her last battle over two decades ago."

"I oversaw the operations that took her and her army down," Vincent confirms. "Everyone on this council—except Trexler—personally witnessed her demise."

"Even if that wench is alive, she's the least of our concerns," Trexler snaps. "Now, if you're done spewing nonsense...?"

"It isn't nonsense." Kasen's voice rises. "She's very alive and has been plotting an attack for years. Worse, she's been doing so right under your noses in the Slum District."

"Do you have proof of this accusation?" Gyra asks. "How can you convince us as to the validity of this knowledge?

"Because..." Kasen gulps down the lump stuck in his throat. The room hovers in complete silence, every face turned in his direction. "I'm from the Slum District," he confesses, all in one breath, and it feels like a stone has fallen from his mouth.

The room floods instantly with gasping, shrieking, ranting, and profanity.

"How can these people be so foul?" Vonnie despairs under the yelling crowd.

"It's how morally corrupted the privileged have become," Sloth comforts her. "To too many of us, anyone even slightly different is an inferior, or even a criminal."

"How dare you defile our academy, Slum?" Trexler shouts. "I demand its immediate execution, and have the corpse hung over the Slum District gates as a warning to all those vermin."

"Calm yourself, Trexler." Gyra says. "Young man, you're aware of the consequences of leaving your district?"

FOREVER WILL END

"I am," Kasen breathes.

"Your Fairest, you mustn't allow this degenerate to speak another word," Trexler scolds him. "How the hell did you get pass the gate? Worthless, pathetic, vile filth!"

"TREXLER." Gyra's bellow scares the room into silence again. "Until we've figured out his motives, I implore you, keep your ill remarks out of this courtroom."

"Forgive me, Your Fairest." Trexler, chastised, sinks back into his seat.

"I was under the impression that Slum District residents are violent criminals, but this boy looks far from it," Vincent observes. "Be reminded he was recruited into the Elite Division, no less."

"Don't be fooled," barks Omar. "That's how they lure you in—before they take things that don't belong to them."

A snarl overcomes Kasen's face as he looks at Omar, glistening in his armor, sitting so high on his seat. Perhaps he only wanted to see a couple of Slum brats make fools of themselves, after all.

"Guess I was so surprised by his performance during the Exams," Omar snorts, "I forgot to do a background check."

"But if he's a Slum resident, then are his accusations true?" asks France.

"What's true is that he's committed a grave crime," Gyra answers.

"She was right," Kasen chuckles in disbelief. "I told you the truth, and all you people care to believe is that I'm a criminal. If I'm your biggest threat, then Chantel shouldn't have a problem attacking the city. Why is it that when I leave the Slum District, it's a capital crime, but when the Higher Ups harass, exploit, kill, and use us for their sick pleasures, you look the other way? I didn't join Legion to ruin your lives. I joined because I'm tired of seeing people I care about suffer for your profit. We Slum residents want Evenrise to be a great civilization just as much as the rest of you, but it won't happen unless we learn to overcome our differences to stop Chantel. There are many in the Slum District who are clinging to life. I can't fail them now that I've come this far. Please. We've suffered enough."

A brief silence turns into hysterical laughter.

"Stupid Slum boy." Trexler wipes away his tears of laughter. "Why would we law-abiding citizens even consider coexisting with your kind? This case is officially a joke."

"Fairest Gyra. His fate rests with you," France says, her calmness quieting the ruckus once more.

"Young man. My heart goes out to you and the residents of the Slum District. I give you my word that the atrocities you've described will be investigated, and those found guilty will be severely punished. However, this doesn't excuse the crimes you've committed, and you will be punished in the manner that the law states. Slum Resident Kasen, for the capital crime of illegally leaving your district, you shall be put to—"

"Time out," Lars coolly interrupts. "Since when does the Fairest Council get off on executing kids?"

"Perhaps you'd like to share his fate?" Trexler threatens.

Gyra eyes Lars from the stands. "Be quick with your words, Second Command."

"You all heard him. Regardless of what you think. Slum residents ARE residents of Evenrise, too. And it's the Legion's sworn duty to protect ALL citizens. Making Legion just as guilty. As a Second Command, I failed to uphold my oath to this city and its people. Kasen's our only reliable source of intelligence on Chantel. You don't have to believe him, but I will. I'll prepare for her attack, but not as a Second Command, or even a Legion soldier. In exchange for a lesser punishment on the accused, I offer my position as payment."

The crowd gasps.

Bronze, silver, gold, and platinum coins—these, Apparitions view more as collectables, not often used in transactions. Apparitions' sense of social worth is instead based mostly upon a citizen's value, lands, titles, and possessions; it was not uncommon occurance that they'd offer their positions, too, as a form of currency. Positions could also be relinquished to avoid criminalization or to reduce the punishment of a crime.

"What do you think you're doing, Lars?" Omar growls.

"I'm not sure." Lars laughs, perplexed, as he rubs his head.

"Has this Slum nonsense brainwashed you?" Trexler shrieks. "You'd wager your position on the word of a criminal?!"

"Perhaps he's overly sympathetic," Vince offers.

"Or an even bigger dumbass than I thought," growls Omar.

"Either way, this is an unexpected turn of events," France, never one to lose her composure, observes.

"Second Command Lars," Gyra begins. "Your expertise on team strategy and your favor among our citizens is what earned you your Second Command position, and had us considering you for a greater role. There isn't any guarantee."

"Then I offer my position, too, whatever it is," Kika shouts.

"You don't have a position," France replies.

"Oh. Never mind. Nice knowing ya, companion."

"Then I," a final voice announces, "offer *mine*."

Ashli. All eyes sweep in trepidation toward where she sits—still and unbothered, Kiera's daughter, the promised Ruler of Evenrise. "Go on," she adds. "Be the fools you are."

"Even you wish to give up your title, Sacred Born?" Gyra asks with astonishment. "The offer must be reviewed by the Fairest Council. We'll reconvene once a verdict has been reached."

At his command, guards move to escort the Fairest Council to a secluded room.

"What just happened?" Kasen mouths.

"A last-ditch effort to save our asses," Lars replies.

"But your position—you shouldn't have."

"Overkill, yeah. But hopefully enough overkill to work."

"And if it doesn't?"

"Hope you know how to function without a head."

With little else to do, they wait in grim silence. Nearly two hours pass before the Fairest Council returns to their seats.

"I refuse to be a part of this case for a second longer." An angry Trexler, obviously flustered by their private communion, stomps out of the courtroom just as soon as he arrives.

Gyra speaks for them all: "After careful consideration of the Second Command and Sacred Born's request, we, the Fairest Council, have come to a just decision." He addresses the pews. "Sacred Born—and I suppose her friend, Kika—shall be suspended from Academy grounds, and forbidden to partake in any Legion activity till further notice. Resident of the Slum District Kasen is to be deported back to his district unharmed. Second Command Lars—or now former Second Command—is to surrender back to Legion all titles and possessions given to him, upon which exchange he will be dishonorably discharged from the Academy, and permanently exiled from Evenrise. These sentences are to be carried out immediately."

Gyra bangs his gavel. Several guards secure Kasen in chains again, readying him to be escorted back to the Slum District. Trexler rushes just behind them, looking, it seems, for any new excuse to have Kasen put down.

"You must've thought you were pretty slick, Slum rat. If I were Fairest, there wouldn't have been a trial. I'd put you down myself," Trexler spits, and the grandeur of Evenrise already feels like a memory as the guards pull Kasen out of the courtroom, and back towards the gate.

"Andre, we have to help." Polina tugs at her husband's arm as they see Kasen walked by the plaza in chains, his head hanging in shame.

"There's nothing we can do," he replies, grim.

Polina refuses to accept it so easily. "But he's just a child!"

"Welcome back to your shithole district," Trexler snarls. Then, to the guards preparing to open the gate: "Be ready to deal harshly with any Slum who gets out of line."

"We're not monsters," Kasen softly says. "All we want are the same opportunities as everyone else."

Trexler yawns. His voice and face couldn't be more sarcastic, or more condemning. "We'll get right on it. Sometime between never and ever."

"Time out again…" Lars arrives with Ashli, Vonnie, and Kika in tow.

"Didn't they exile you, traitor?" Trexler snaps. "This is official Legion business."

"I'll be out of your hair as soon as you hand over Kasen."

"I don't want to trouble anyone anymore. I'll just…continue being a Slum resident," Kasen supposes.

"Yeah. About that. I mean, you could if you were a Slum resident—but you can't, because you're also exiled."

"What?!" Trexler shrieks.

"We're going on an adventure, companion," Kika chirps.

"Or you can simply roll over and die," Ashli offers, just in case Kasen wasn't aware of that option.

"I told you I had a plan—sort of. The Fairest Council granted me one request before I departed," Lars tells him. "You want to fight? Well, this is your shot, and given your situation, it's not like you have a better option."

"This can't be legal. I'm going to speak with the Fairest this instant." Trexler storms off.

"He's your problem now," a guard mutters, uncaring. His fellows unchain Kasen and, disinterested, depart.

Kasen isn't so sure. His eyes linger on the dark gate. "But the Slum District…"

"I'll look after them, Kasen." Vonnie promises. "We also have Andre, Polina, and many in the Commoners District. What we're fighting for has become much bigger than what we've set out to do. We can't let Chantel win—not anymore."

"What do you say, kid? With you three under my wing—figuratively speaking—we'll take Chantel down, no sweat," Lars assures with a wing/thumbs up.

"It's like you said, Lars. I don't have much of a choice, now that I'm exiled."

ELITES-IN-TRAINING (AGAIN)

L ars takes his exiled team of Kasen, Ashli, and Kika to the Centraland Outskirts, a series of connected village towns consisting mainly of farmers, ranchers, and retired soldiers who wanted the quiet life. The villages had been under Evenrise's protection, but since the city's reform, they've been the victims of constant Feral raids. Now their homes lie in ruin. As they see Lars's team draw closer, several denizens hide behind the rubble of their once-houses.

"Make yourselves at home," Lars casually says as Kasen, Ashli, and Kika look upon the desolated town.

"What happened here?" asks Kasen.

"It's what happens when you stop upholding your oath," Lars says. "What we're going to do is rebuild their homes and village and protect it from those pesky Feral. So like Evenrise, but better."

"And the point of this is?" Ashli asks.

"Sense of accomplishment, mostly." Lars points to a massive stack of piled tree trunks. "I've had a team out here trying to rebuild the village, until Evenrise ordered all troops back to the city. You three will start hauling the trunks over near the ruined homes, followed by whatever else I tell you to do. Let's get to work."

"How are we supposed to carry these?" The tree trunks Lars indicated are as wide as Kasen's wingspan and weigh more than he can lift.

"Try using your pinky." Lars chuckles.

"I think I like this game." Kika effortlessly lifts a trunk up over her head, carries it over to one of the ruined houses, and throws it down at a few villagers' feet.

"You were supposed to catch that." They look at her in confusion. She rolls her eyes. "Fine, I'll get another."

Try as he might, Kasen can hardly get a trunk off the ground.

"You look ridiculous," Ashli says. She lifts the opposite end of the trunk, making things easier.

The three stack tree trunks from morning to well into the afternoon. Kasen never recalled Chantel making him work this hard. Every part of him feels sore. He can smell his own foulness, the sting of sweat in the cuts on his arms, hands and legs. It soon becomes too much. Succumbing to fatigue, Kasen falls to his hands and knees.

"C'mon, companion. Don't tell me you're done playing." Kika balances a trunk on her head. Ashli had since retreated from labor to adopt a meditative pose.

"How are you guys not tired?' Kasen pants.

"She's right—villages don't build themselves." Lars relaxes over a tree branch. He hasn't lifted a finger since they started. "We can always watch Evenrise burn to the ground instead. We basically have front row seats. I'll even bring snacks."

Kasen mumbles. He claws at the ground beneath him. Fighting against his pain, he stands.

"I still fail to see how any of this is our problem in the first place," Ashli says. "It's not like any amount of preparation will do him any good."

"Did you only bring me here to bash me?" Kasen growls as he shuffles over to the stack of trunks. "Go ahead and laugh; I'll prove you all wrong." He lifts one side of a trunk high enough so he can at least drag it. "I'll do it myself," Kasen snaps at Ashli, just in case she intends to assist him again.

The labor continues until sunset. But even then, Kasen refuses to rest. He has to member how to summon the black sword like he did before. He would never be controlled again.

"Do you know how late it is, kid?" Lars yawns.

"Sorry. I'll go to sleep soon. I'm just trying to figure something out."

"Geez. You stern types make me nervous."

"Lars. Did I really make Chantel retreat? When I was 'possessed,' or whatever it was. Could she have been defeated?"

"At most, I'd say you caught her off guard. Hell, you caught us all off guard. That's some serious weapon power you have on you. But if you want to put Chantel down, you should get a better grip on how to use it."

"Yeah." Kasen doesn't need to be reminded again.

"Do you think of yourself as a leader?" Lars wonders.

"What do you mean by that?"

"Let's take Ashli and Kika, for instance. We all know they're way higher up on the ability scale than you. I don't know what Kika's on, but the Sacred Born has a natural talent. But that doesn't mean either are capable leaders. Leaders are people who motivate and inspire others. They fuel their followers with hope and confidence, even in dire circumstances. But they make mistakes just like anyone else. Their job is to maintain a cool head. If they fall apart, so do those who follow them. You've stood against Chantel when I couldn't. You knew she was more skilled. You'll need to hold on to that confidence from here-on-out. Understand?"

Kasen nods. "I think so."

"Good enough." Lars stretches his wings upward. His shirt lifts enough to reveal a tattoo near his hip.

"What's that?" Kasen points. Though he isn't able to get a solid look at it, the shape is eerily familiar; it reminds him of the symbol on Chantel's crates.

"What's what?" When Lars realizes what Kasen is pointing at, he quickly pulls his shirt down. "Oh! That was from wilder times. Peer pressure, wanting to fit in, and one very bad hangover." He laughs. "Anyhow, goodnight." And he quickly walks off.

In a short period of time, Kasen, Ashli, and Kika work rigorously to restore the desolated villages. And it doesn't go unnoticed. As the sun rises to a new morning, Kasen is woken by panic and bustling. Women secure their children; men rummage for anything that might be used as a weapon. Lars, for his part, tries to calm the villagers with limited success.

"Companion. Can he play with us, too?" Kika points to a lone Feral approaching from the distance on horseback.

"Damn these Feral. Today we fight back." A villager rallies the others to agree.

"By the looks of it, he's only a messenger. Meaning a camp of who-knows-how-many are close by. We'll have to convince them they're wasting time on us; hopefully they'll move on."

"Since when do Feral move on?" Ashli challenges.

Lars sighs. "Well, not everything can be fixed by plunging a sword through it."

"It's worked so far."

"Everyone just chill for a sec," Lars orders sharply. "Drop your sticks and stones and just let me do the talking."

The townsfolk begrudgingly obey as the Feral gets off their horse. A rough-looking type, like most.

"Welcome." Lars's greeting is polite. "What brings you to our ruined settlement?"

The Feral ignores him, snorting and grunting as they inspect the village folk and the rebuilding progress.

"Er. As you can see, most of our resources have already been plunder by Feral, so…"

"Who you callin' 'Feral,' ya scrawny shit?" The Feral gets in Lars face. Lars inhales the stench coming off them. "You think we're some damn wild animals? Answer me, scrawny shit."

"I meant no offense. I always thought of it as show of respect," Lars answers.

"The Band of Rouges isn't a pack of rabid animals and if you don't want anything rabid tearing out your guts, keep your mouth shut."

"He got shown-up like a bitch," Kika whispers to Kasen.

The Feral returns his attention to the townsfolk. "This village now belongs to The Rouges. If ya want to keep livin', then keep on building, and by that I mean hurry the fuck up."

A villager confronts the Feral. "These are our homes. What gives you the right to take them?"

The villager is struck to the ground. The others gasp, but it's the whimpering of a little girl that gets the Feral's attention. Her mother shields her from the attacker's view.

"Oh, yeah. The boss told me to bring back a youngin' for him."

"Stay away, monster!" The father attacks. He's caught by the neck and head-butted until his face is bloody. His wife and children go quickly to his aid.

"That's enough!" Kasen shouts. The Feral releases the villager and confronts him, instead. "Got a problem with how I run things?"

"What you're doing to these people is wrong, and you know it. This should be an opportunity for us to work together to create something for everyone. These people already have nothing, so why continue tormenting them?"

The Feral bellows. "Here's what gonna happen, hotshot. Everyone here's gonna do what I say. Every child's going back to the boss, but before that, I'm gonna kill ya, stuff ya, and incinerate your stuffed corpse."

The Feral pulls out a rusted knife and prepare to stick Kasen. The black sword appears unexpectedly. It's long enough to impale the Feral immediately. Kasen's face fills with horror; his body trembles at the site of the Feral's cringe. Kasen pulls the sword out, and throws it to the ground.

The Feral spits a few last words before collapsing: "Fucking. Bastard."

Kasen looks at his hands. They shake under the blood of his victim. *"You're not a killer. You're not Chantel,"* he insists to himself. Fearing what the witnesses might think of him, he flees from the village and into the woods.

Reaching a stream, Kasen angrily washes the red stain from his hands. He desperately wants to believe this is a bad dream.

"What have I done?" Kasen is in disarray. "I wanted to settle things peacefully, and the sword… Why did it kill him? That's not who I am."

"Found ya again, companion." It doesn't take long for Kika and Lars to catch up to him.

"You alright, kid?"

"What's happening to me?" Kasen sobs. "I know that Feral was a terrible person, but I didn't mean for them to die."

"You didn't do anything wrong. That Feral was a freak. If anything, they made the mistake by coming out this way."

"That's not the point. I'm tired of seeing people die." Kasen cries. "How can I stop that from happening when I can't even control my actions?"

"Cheer up, companion." Kika consoles him. "You may have killed someone against your will, but at least you didn't cheat while playing a game, because that's unforgivable."

"Quit babying him." Ashli arrives with the black sword clutched in her hand. "A mis-educated boy who desperately wants to change the world, but easily breaks down over the most trivial matters. If he can't wrap his head around the fact that this is war, then perhaps he'd function better without it."

Ashli attacks Kasen with the black sword, leaving a slash mark over his arm. Unlike the fight with Omar, the black sword wounds him.

"This isn't funny, Ashli!" Kasen yells, turning to Lars and Kika for help.

"She has a point, you know," Lars replies.

"I'm gonna say 'bitch,' because I can't think of a better word," says Kika.

"Even your companion agrees. Now hold still." Ashli attacks Kasen again, landing a cut to his leg.

"Wish we had something to eat," Kika mumbles to Lars in the interim. "Think she'll kill him?"

"Hard to tell. If there's a lesson to be learned, Kasen better learn it fast."

"Accept how useless you are and die." Ashli closes in for the finishing attack.

As she does, Kasen hears a faint and familiar voice in his head, one that reminded him of a very important promise he made. He reaches out his hand; the black sword disappears from Ashli's, and retakes its spot in Kasen's. He can feel his strength returning—perhaps even growing. A moment of forgetting his promise, and the black sword disappears, and reappears upon remembering it again.

"Think I'm starting to see what's going on," Lars says. "Seems that fancy sword of yours only appears under the right circumstances. Such as imminent danger to you or someone close to you. At least that's what I'm gathering. It could explain why it's been acting against Kasen's will."

"What? No way," Kika shoots down. "That's impossible. Is it?"

"Just a theory. But at least you're getting the hang of it now."

"That's right," Kasen insists. "I told you I'd prove you wrong, and now I'll show you how wrong."

He charges Ashli. His inexperience in battle is easily exploited by a gut-wrenching fist.

'Again? Seriously. This is getting old.' Crumpling to his knees, Kasen coughs, huffs, and heaves once more.

"That even hurt me a little," Lars winces out. Kika laughs hysterically.

"Now you're reckless," Ashli observes, then issues a cold warning: "Suppose I'll let you continue humoring yourself for the time being, but the moment you give me such a pitiful display again will be your last moment."

Kasen pants. "R—Right."

They leave the riverside and, eventually, resume rebuilding efforts as normal. Under Lars's close instruction, Kasen improves in most every aspect. The Feral, they know, will return with every intention to take over the villages, and Kasen plans to use every new advantage to prevent that dark day.

The disruption of exile settled in the city Evenrise. The gates of the Slum District had been heavily modified to prevent any more escapes. Several new signs hang over them, warning the Slum residents of the consequences promised after disobeying the law.

Though it had become more difficult, none of this stopped Vonnie from regularly supplying the District with food—the city patrol guards were still as lazy as they had always been.

Beyond the Slums, newly-elected council member Trexler had made it a personal mission to make life harder for non-Higher Ups. Commoners now had to abide by a mandatory curfew, and anyone suspected of sympathizing with Slumfolk—or unlucky enough to be caught after-hours—was immediately deported to the Slum District.

"What the hell's this supposed to be?" Trexler spits a mouthful of salad on his personal gourmand.

"The salad you requested, my lord," answers the gourmand dutifully.

"Worst I've ever tasted. Guards, deport this poor excuse of a gourmand to the Slum District immediately."

The chef resists the grabbing mitts of the guards. "I haven't committed a crime!"

"Failing to make a simple salad. For all I know, it's dressed with poison. Get this degenerate out of my sight."

The chef is dragged away.

"Keeping the peace is hard work." Trexler wipes his brow. "When Evenrise becomes a crime-free civilization, the people will have me to thank. I can already see it." He imagines himself being hailed by the citizens as the new Fairest of Evenrise. Turned on by his fantasy, he fondles himself.

"Excuse me, Lord Trexler. You have a visitor." His assistant awkwardly interrupts, looking away from Trexler's private moment.

"I'm not expecting visitors," Trexler snaps in annoyance. "Tell them to leave, or they'll be added to those deported today."

"Apologies, my lord, but this one knows you by name and is very persistent."

A ram Bizarre moves the assistant aside.

"Leave. Now!" Trexler shrieks at his assistant, and they scurry away. Trexler watches as the ram gobbles down his salad.

"Disgusting," he notes, swallowing the last leaf, and belches loudly. That said, he rummages through Trexler's things, throwing anything unappealing to the floor.

"Garrick. What a pleasant surprise." Trexler's voice trembles. "What brings you here…now?"

"Trexler. I'd thought you'd be thrilled to see the guy who got you on your high horse." Garrick places his hand on Trexler's shoulder, making him flinch. He gives the shoulder a friendly squeeze. "We're good friends, right?"

"I…erm…yes?"

"Good. Because I want us to have a friendly conversation." Garrick grabs Trexler by his neck, drags him out of his chair, and pins him against the wall. "Why are you screwing me over?" he roars. "We had a deal. You'd keep your Legion goons away from the Centralands and I wouldn't easily take over the city."

"I—did—what—asked." Trexler can barely speak.

"So why are my men still having problems with Legion?"

"They were ordered to be pulled back. There shouldn't be any…!" It is only now that Trexler realizes whom Garrick must be talking about about. "I—swear—I—can—fix—this."

Garrick laughs before releasing his throat.

"Come on, we're friends. You really thought I was gonna kill ya?" Garrick pats Trexler. "I'm sure you'll make things right. And from one friend to another, we best not have this conversation again."

Garrick leaves Trexler alone in his chambers with an empty salad bowl.

"This time," Trexler snarls. "There won't be a trial."

UNITE & ACHIEVE

oday, the Higher Ups of Evenrise celebrate the anniversary of their great city's founding.

Children listen to folktales of triumph over warlord adversaries and play games in the streets. Adults nibble on unappealing snacks and drink until their words slur. But for Legion's guards, it's just another day on patrol.

A group positioned at the main gates is engaged in a game of cards—the loser of which will have to make rounds. Normally, their rounds involve merely glancing at the lands beyond the city with a scope. This time, however, a second glance spots several Feral standing in the open field.

A ram Bizarre aims his crossbow and fires a bolt that shatters the guard's telescope, sticking deep into their socket. The other guards look up from their game just in time to see their comrade fall dead, and hear the Feral attackers send up a rallying shout.

Cries of battle ring in the air. The guards ascend the main gates to see hundreds of Feral charging for the city.

"I thought you said you'd help me awaken my inner power." Vonnie is in the middle of a training session with Sloth. They'd normally hold sessions in the same area where she had taken her exam, or any well-shaded spot.

"Learning to channel and control Aura is an important step," he replies.

Vonnie grumbles. "Well, if I knew it was this tedious, I would've reconsidered your offer."

"Enough complaining, young lady. Now focus."

Vonnie does as instructed; her eyes shut and mind concentrates. A light pink Aura glows around her.

"No form of training is ever tedious." Sloth circles Vonnie. "You'll be disciplined in every requirement, no matter how simple or complex. The tide of battle can shift in an instant and your mind must always be ready to anticipate changes."

Vonnie gives in to the strain of her focus. The Aura around her subsides.

Sloth doesn't seem disappointed—or surprised. "We'll rest a moment before resuming."

"I can't wait to show Kasen how much I've improved," Vonnie boasts. "Maybe I'll be strong enough to stop Chantel myself. What do you think, Sloth?" She waits for his answer, but sees that her Commander's mind is drawn to something else. His gaze is fixed beyond Academy grounds.

Soon come the sounds of screams and swords clashing. Sounds that make Vonnie's heart race.

"Wait here," Sloths tells her.

"But I'm ready," Vonnie argues.

"That's exactly what someone who isn't ready would say. Find a safe place to hide quickly."

Begrudgingly, Vonnie hides as Sloth makes haste to the battlefield.

"Your stance is still weak." Lars is instructing Kasen in the finer points of combat.

"My stance?" he parrots.

"I think he means your standing sucks," says Kika.

Kasen looks at his feet. "What's wrong with the way I stand?"

"Idiot," grumbles Ashli as the three interrupt her meditation.

It's far from the last interruption of the day. Soon after, a villager runs up to their training site, informing Lars that Legion Soldiers are en route.

"Hey, companion! It's that guy that hates you a lot." Kika points toward the approaching force.

"Oh, shit." Lars sees that Trexler—of all people—is leading them. "We've got company, kids."

They near the village quickly. Trexler, on foot, looks furious to be so far away from the comforts of home.

"Morning, soldiers of Evenrise. What brings you lot to the Outskirts?" Lars greets them like a friend.

"Not a bad job restoring the villages, exiles." Trexler sneers. "But wouldn't it look better if they were burned to the ground?"

"Why didn't we think of that?" Kika hums.

"I thought I wouldn't have to deal with you criminals anymore, but even I can be merciful if the situation calls for it." Trexler turns to Ashli. "Sacred Born. Your role in Evenrise is too pivotal for you to simply disregard it. Even your obnoxious friend could prove useful, if she was better disciplined. You must be rid of this Slum filth who has brainwashed you. Second Command Larson, it's not too late. Come back to Evenrise with your crimes pardoned and your rank restored."

"What have Slum residents done to make you hate them so much?" Kasen snaps.

"Silence, cretin," Trexler snaps back. "This is your last chance, Sacred Born. End your association with this undignified life-form this instant!"

"I side with no one." Ashli only now stands from her meditation.

"I don't think you've noticed, Trex," says Lars, "but no one really likes you."

"And I'm gonna say..." Kika says. *"Bitch."*

"You've the nerve to insult a member of the Fairest Council? I see no Sacred Born. Only a false Ruler and pitiful sympathizers. Enemies of Evenrise will be shown no mercy."

"Run away!" shouts a panicking Evenrise guard, interrupting Trexler before he can command his men to attack.

"What are you doing outside the city?" Trexler snaps.

"Feral—attack—city. Too many. Couldn't fight," the fleeing guard manages between huffs.

"That's impossible. Feral wouldn't dare attack Evenrise." Trexler's voice is wrathful and certain, but in truth, his face looks less-sure.

"We have to help them," blurts Kasen. The looks on Ashli and Kika's face say different.

"Or how about, instead, we don't," Kika suggests.

"Have you forgotten those same fools you wish to save wanted you executed?" Ashli reminds him. "Let irony be their demise."

"It's time to be a leader. What will you do now, lad?" Lars wonders.

"Kika. We're supposed to be companions, right? You wouldn't want me going on a dangerous adventure by myself? And Ashli, this battle can be your chance to show everyone what you're capable of."

"Is that all?' Ashli asks, not looking remotely convinced.

"Yes?"

At Kasen's response, Ashli simply walks past him.

"C'mon, companion—before you're left behind." Kika follows after Ashli—and, in turn, Kasen follows after them. And the three make haste for Evenrise.

"Where do you think you're going? You're all exiled traitors. Returning to Evenrise warrants the death penalty," Trexler shrieks, and whirls around to his men. "I didn't bring you out here to stand around like idiots. Go kill them!"

"Sorry to be the bearer of obvious news," one answers, glancing uneasily to his cohorts. "But REALLY, no one likes you. Let's go save our home, boys."

"I will not stand for this insubordination. You'll all be facing execution." Trexler can only shout at his men's backs as they head for Evenrise, as well.

"Oh, Trex." Lars begins to pop the bones in his wings and neck. "I think we should have a little chat."

"Damn, this is too easy," Garrick says as he breaks a Legion soldier's neck.

He and his men have little trouble breaching the city. Many guards lie slain through the streets; those still able flee for their lives. Scores of citizens, forced to fend for themselves, are taken hostage. Despite his best efforts, Sloth, too, is captured; the loss of their Commanders throws the armies of Evenries into disarray, leaving them scattered and too unorganized to initiate a proper counterattack.

"Good morning, Evenrise!" Garrick stands before the lot of weeping hostages as his Feral subordinates move through the crowd, placing explosive-packed jackets on their prisoners while the sacking of Evenrise commences. They had tarnished the festive theme streets of the Higher Up district. "Let me start by introducing myself—"

"Savage Feral beast. You won't get away with—" A hostage's outburst is cut short with an arrow bolt into their neck. Panic sweeps through the others.

"Do not interrupt; it's rude. As I was going to say: My name's Garrick. I lead these fine men. We're a pleasant group who march under the banner of the Band of Rouges. We were once proud citizens and soldiers of your precious civilization. Until that all changed when your leaders reformed into a group of pansy-asses dedicated only to your social laws. Long story short, we're here to reclaim our homes."

"Let me go!" Vonnie claws at the Feral carrying her over their shoulder. She's tossed with the rest of the hostages.

"I'm gonna need you to settle down, little girl," Garrick tells her.

"You've made a big mistake." Vonnie bravely locks eyes with him. "Once my friends come, they'll make you regret attacking the city."

"Could someone shut her up?" Garrick signals to his men. One fires a crossbow bolt that flies just over Vonnie and plunges into the hostage knelt beside her.

"Oops, I missed" The Feral laughs. "Guess I'll have to randomly fire again..."

"No, please," Vonnie cries as panic swells among the hostages again.

"Good girl." Garrick pats Vonnie's head. "Where's the cavalry, already? I mean, how many more do I need to kill to get a proper audience?"

At his words, the Elite Division arrives en mass, surrounding the Band of Rogues.

Omar confronts him. "You're still the same old Garrick."

"Omar? No shit?" If the growling voice wasn't enough of a giveaway, a glimpse of his armor makes the Commander's identity clear. "You all remember Omar, boys." Garrick's men snicker. "You really have to see it to believe. You're standing on the wrong side of the battlefield, friend."

"It's over. You're out-manned and outmatched. Release the hostages and surrender, Feral," Jaq demands. Her bow aims for Garrick's head.

"Will you quit calling us that?" Garrick snaps. "Omar. We go way back. Even you'd know that I wouldn't do something unless I was sure it'd work out."

Nodding to one another, many Elite Legion soldiers turn on their comrades, either cutting them down or disarming them. The rebels surround Omar and Jaq, forcing them to their knees.

"Age really has caught up with you if you can't even recognize your own men anymore." Garrick unsheathes his sickle. "There's a nice-sized bounty on your head, but I'm guessing you already knew that."

"You, cut me down?" Omar laughs. "You couldn't cut butter with a hacksaw."

"Then you won't mind me trying."

As Garrick readies to decapitate Omar, the sounds of battle grow louder. Before the executions can conclude, Kasen—along with Trexler's men—fight their way through a cluster of Feral insurgents and burst into the huddled circle of hostages.

"That obnoxious Slum boy again," Omar growls.

"Was a dramatic entry necessary?" Garrick sighs. "How many did you kill just to get to me? And you call *us* Feral."

"These people haven't done anything to you. Release them," Kasen demands. He doesn't want to attack unless it comes down to it. Garrick simply laughs.

"That's it?"

"Release them or else," Kasen warns.

"You seem to be new at this whole hostage negotiation thing." Garrick's men chuckle as their leader turns to face the captive Commander. "Omar. Is this little punk really your last line of defense? He's not even wearing a uniform."

"I don't need to be a soldier to do what's right," Kasen insists.

Garrick hoists Vonnie by her collar. "These your friends you were boasting about a second ago? You see that man atop the building?" Garrick points, watching Kasen's eyes follow his finger. "Once I give the signal, he'll blast these hostages straight to hell. So you can either drop your weapons and get on your knees like a good little bastard, or spend the remainder of your life cleaning their entrails off the streets.

"I'm not warning you again." Kasen raises his sword threateningly—at which Garrick laughs.

"You've got more balls than anyone here. I'll give you that much. Cleaning up the streets, it is." He signals the man overhead to detonate the explosives.

Nothing.

Garrick is baffled, and gestures another time, but it's no more useful than the first. He waits for carnage that never arrives. Kasen, however, understands immediately. Ashli had long since slain the tech.

"Take back the city," Omar shouts as he seizes a Feral's face and hurls their body into a group of infiltrators standing by.

Jaq slams the back of her head into the Feral standing behind her, takes their sidearm, and stabs them dead. She quickly grabs the misplaced bow off the ground and shoots down the scrambling soldiers.

"Cowards. Can't even finish what they start." Omar grumbles, as Feral—now facing real opposition—scatter and flee for their lives.

"Took you long enough." Vonnie gives Kasen a friendly tap. He replies with a smile.

Those soldiers still loyal to Evenrise hurriedly remove the explosive jackets and clear freed hostages away from the battlefield. As his men are slain around him, Garrick scurries into the alleys to plot a hasty escape.

He runs right into Kika.

"Hello, person I've never met before. Have you seen my companion, and do you possibly have something to eat?"

"Yeah, I have something you'll enjoy. You ever wanted to travel?" Garrick maliciously grins.

"Hey, companion. This guy wants to talk to you." Kika, with Garrick holding her at crossbow-point, appears from the alleys.

"Very clever to hide Malik's daughter in the one place we couldn't reach her," he spits. "I'll be leaving the city. I'm not to be harmed or be followed, and I'm taking this jewel piece with me."

"That's Malik's daughter?" Omar gasps.

"Her capture is just as rewarding as taking this city. Once she's handed over to her buyers, I'll return with a mass army. And no one will dare look down on the Band of Rouges again."

"But you're the tall one. So we technically look up to you," Kika points out.

"Quiet, freak." Garrick moves to strike her. Before his hand connects, Kika's survival instincts trigger; her eyes flare violet as she jabs her elbow into Garrick's abdomen, leaving a gruesome hole.

"Ew. I can see your gut…guts?" Kika seems to have no recollection of what she's just done as the flare in her eyes fades.

Garrick hacks blood. Omar hoists him by the neck and pins him against the wall.

"Omar," he chokes, splattering red. "It doesn't make a damn difference if you kill me. The Sigil has regrouped the Armies of Evil. You're all going to die."

"At least you we won't be dealing with the likes of you anymore."

Omar breaks Garrick's neck, and drops his limp, motionless body.

Civil unrest fills the streets of Evenrise over the next few days. The citizens are convinced that huddling in the inner city is no longer safer than living outside the city. Soldiers blockade the Academy as protesters demand new and trustworthy leadership. The sounds of their cries even reach the Council chambers.

"Were you going to inform me our military was *lacking* in some aspects?" or so Vincent begins his assembly with the Fairest Council.

"This is news to me, Lord Commander," France replies. "My Medical Division has been working nonstop to heal the injured."

"They should be on their knees with gratitude that we saved their asses," Omar growls.

"That aside," Gyra steers, "we can't ignore Garrick's warning. The Sigil is creating trouble once more."

Vincent's prediction is dark. "When they receive word that Evenrise was almost taken by a minor Feral group, they won't bother with a strategy. They'll just start destroying everything they can reach."

"I wanted to believe the policies we established would keep the citizens of Evenrise safe," Gyra continues, heavy with the weight of the city threatening to crumble around them. "Now our enemies know they can attack Evenrise whenever they choose, and with minimal casualties. If something doesn't change, we are doomed."

"How do you suppose we change things, Your Fairest?" France asks.

"Excuse me. But I think we may have a way to help you." The Fairest Councilors look up to see Kasen, Vonnie, Andre, and Polina standing at chamber doors.

"Do you always barge in unwelcomed, Slum boy?" Omar barks. "Legion thanks you for your assistance in the raid, but that doesn't change the fact that you're still exiled."

"That's enough, Elite Commander," Gyra calmly intervenes. "Andre. Polina."

Andre nods. "Good to see you again, old friend."

After a few hours of speaking with their guests, the Fairest Council decides to stand before the public. They are greeted with all manner of profanity.

"Citizens of Evenrise, please allow us to speak." Gyra shouts over them. A moment passes before the angry crowd quiets down. "Today marks an error made by the Fairest Council. We've convinced ourselves— and you—that our social structure is the perfect means to maintain order and keep the peace. But our enemies still lurk in the shadows. They aim to destroy the city. Slums, Commoners, AND Higher Ups. They prepare for all-out war against Evenrise. But we won't be the Evenrise that the world has since come to know. We'll be a great, strong, united civilization. If we learn to put aside our differences and adjust—if we can live, work, and grow hand-in-hand—I promise you our enemies will have a much more difficult time taking Evenrise from you. If you truly wish to protect your homes and families, we must put aside our statuses and the titles we've given ourselves. Only then will Evenrise be triumphant."

Silence became slow clapping—and then, eventually, cheers, as both Higher Ups and Commoners joined together to show support.

Over a few months time, Evenrise endures major changes. The gates of the Slum District are torn down. The Higher Ups who have more than they need are encouraged to donate what they can. Everyone is offered the privilege of becoming a Legion soldier if they choose to. The army undergoes retraining. The rift between the classes slowly thins.

Trexler, meanwhile—knowing that if he returns to Evenrise, he'll be exposed for working alongside Feral—flees into the caves of the Uncharted Territories. Where he finds himself face-to-face with a familiar threat.

"Please. I did everything you asked of me." Trexlor pleads before Chantel, Juan, and Yuan. "I convinced the Band of Rouges they could take Evenrise; I earned the trust of the Fairest Council and convinced them to pull their armies away from their strongholds. Everything was going according to plan until that little Slum shit came out of nowhere and ruined everything," he snarls.

"Ugh. Will you stop worrying over nothing?" Chantel yawns and stretches.

"You should get a massage." Juan jumps at Yuan's touch. "Hey, that's not my back."

"Sorry. Sometimes I can't help where my hands go." Yuan giggles.

Chantel, Juan, and Yuan had settled in a cave hidden in the mountains of the Uncharted Territory. Caves—and this cave had a comfortable amount of space to spend days in, even weeks—were always the preferred hiding locations for Feral.

"My lady. Then why put me through all this effort?" Trexler begs. "Legion was already a weak military. Very few know of your whereabouts. What good are savage Feral, anyways? You knew they couldn't pull it off."

"Evenrise cut down a few Feral—it only means less work on our end. Let them bask in their empty victory. It just brings them that much closer to their demise."

NOBLE AFFAIR

"**T**hank you for taking time to meet with the Fairest Council, Edwin." Gyra begins the council meeting by welcoming the young Noble lord.

"I'm honored to stand before the council," Edwin humbly replies. "Trexler wasn't found among the slain. A tragedy."

"The reason we've summoned you is your knowledge of the Uncharted Territories. The Feral will be a constant nuisance so long as they hold camps there," says Vincent.

"And I've grown tired of letting the Feral have a hole to crawl back into," growls Omar. "We need to get rid of them at the source."

"The knowledge you posses is crucial enough to be seated with us in the Council—if that is what you wish," France offers.

"I'm honored." Edwin politely bows. "I'd be more than willing to assist the council in these crucial times. There may just be a way to tip the odds in our favor."

"I'm just saying: Why doesn't our companion have any guy friends? Makes you wonder," Kika muses to Vonnie. They—along with many others from Evenrise—are busy reestablishing raided settlements outside of the city.

"Wonder what?"

"I can't be the only one noticing," Kika says, astounded. Ashli, in meditation, deeply sighs, bothered by their conversation. "Our companion's obviously—"

"You've got a visitor, kids," yells Lars as a young and beautiful woman of a light-yellow hue, dressed in a her business uniform, politely gestures to them.

"Good afternoon." Her voice is soothing. "I'm Melony. I represent Evenrise's well-respected Nobles."

"You're hot. Don't you agree, companion?" Kika nudges Kasen.

"I...uh." He stammers in reply, blushing. He's glad he is lost for words—otherwise he'd be sure to make things even more awkward.

"Um. Thanks?" Melony winces at the awkward meeting. "Lord Edwin's tasked me with extending invitations to Evenrise's new heroes to attend a special banquet at his manor this evening. Wardrobes will be provided to you." She hands Kasen, Ashli, and Kika invitations with Edwin's signature stamp.

"I don't think I'd fit in well with Nobles," Kasen notes.

"Waste of time," says Ashli.

"And I'm Kika...I mean, no."

"You mean yes," Lars corrects them. "You agreed to build a better Evenrise. So that means you'll be doing things you don't want to."

"Think of it as an opportunity," Vonnie suggests. "There may be some who aren't convinced."

"Suppose it couldn't hurt." Even as he relents, Kasen knows he'll regret his decision come tonight.

"So it's a date, then," Lars confirms. "Wrap it up for the day; you've been working too hard, and some of you hardly at all."

"Must you concern yourself with everything?" Ashli asks Kasen coldly as they all-together return to the city.

"Sorry."

"Kids these days, am I right?" Lars asks Melony. She hands him a scroll with Edwin and the Fairest Council's stamp.

"This was to be given to you."

Edwin's servants are already waiting for Kasen, Ashli, and Kika to return to Evenrise. They give them separate packages containing the wardrobes they are to wear tonight.

"I feel...off," Kasen admits, returning sheepishly to his friends after changing into a zebra-patterned vest and pants. The leather shoes pinch at his ankles.

"I think you look stylish, companion." Kika flounces in her glittering sequin dress and lily hat.

"I just hope this is a one-time-only kind of thing," grumbles Kasen.

"Well, you're no fun. Hey, Ash. Don't you think our companion looks stylish?"

As Ashli steps from her dressing room, Kasen and Kika's jaws drop. Her white silk dress is dipped with blue waves streaming along the bottom; her necklace and earrings are made of pearl. The left front of her hair is nearly curled, and the back drawn into a messy ponytail that is truly anything but messy. It is though this night is just for her.

"Hot damn," Kika says in awe.

"You're beautiful," Kasen wanted to say.

"Let's get this over with," Ashli counters quickly, and so they do.

The Nobles of Evenrise dwell within a separate neighborhood (often called Noblehood) established across the river, beside the Academy. Those foolish enough to try swimming across would find themselves pulled under by its current. The only means of crossing into Noblehood was by raft.

Edwin's manor stood on a hilltop, and in preparation for the banquet, its yard and rooftops are fluttering with Legion banners. At the entrance, servants greet and escort the attending Nobles inside. It is an elderly servant that quickly tends to Kasen, Ashli, and Kika.

"Lady Ashli, Lady Kika, and Young Master Kasen. Lord Edwin thanks you for accepting his invitation. I'm his castellan, Wilbert, at your service. We're honored to welcome you to Lord Edwin's home."

Edwin's manor is better-decorated than Legion Academy. Portraits of their host and other significant Apparitions hang on the walls, chandeliers upon on the ceiling. Wilbert leads the three to the ballroom, where the Nobles gather. They converse and sip on fine vintage. Rows of tables boast hors d'oeuvres decoratively placed around marble sculptures. On stage, an orchestra plays soft ballroom jazz. Servants scurry through the partygoers, refilling any empty glass they see.

"Lord Edwin apologizes for not welcoming you himself. Surely you'll become acquainted before the night's end. If there's anything more you need, don't hesitate to ask." Wilbert bows before leaving.

"So, this is what the other side of life looks like. Must be nice to have everything," Kasen envies.

"You ever get tired of moping?" Ashli coldly asks.

Kika sighs. "Will you two ever get along?"

"Doubt it," Kasen and Ashli both answer.

A spoon tapping against glass directs attention to Melony on stage. She's traded her uniform for a bright blue and scarlet dress.

"Ladies and gentlemen, dearly invited guests. Thank you for gathering to celebrate a historic night. Please join me in welcoming your host for this evening, Lord Edwin." The Nobles clap as two stunning ladies holding the arms of a dashing young man in an all-white tuxedo take center stage. Women who couldn't find a date for tonight stare enviously at the lucky ladies, but even those who had come with one look a little jealous.

"Thank you, Melony." Edwin begins as the applause fades. "As many of you know, it was my father and grandfather who most contributed to the construction of our glorious Evenrise. They dreamt up a society where law, order, and morality prevailed over savagery. Their unfortunate passing has left me to finish their life's work. Today I'm proud to say their dreams have become reality." The Nobles lightly clap. "These efforts weren't accomplished by one man. It's the loyalty, support, and love you bear for our community that keeps us thriving. We've learned to accept and embrace others—those slightly and even vastly different than ourselves. Over these months passed, Evenrise has become more united than we've ever imagined. You'll agree that the world should know how strong we are as a united civilization. As tonight, Legion Academy shall henceforth be known as The Academy of United Apparitions!"

Blue and black banners roll from the ceiling, emblazoned with the bold *U.A.* abbreviation over a a seven-pointed star. The Nobles cheer.

"I'm pleased that that you approve. Now, let the merriment resume."

The orchestra resumes its music, and the Nobles resume their chattering.

"Well, that was the most boring thing ever. I'm gonna play explorer now. Bye!" Kika dashes off.

"That was…something." Kasen turns to see Ashli has isolated herself in the farthest corner.

"Hors d'oeuvres?" A servant presents Kasen with a platter of blue chips containing a black jelly paste. Not wanting to be rude, he regrettably takes one into his mouth and immediately spits out the awful taste. He receives horrid looks from a pair of Nobles walking past.

"Oh... hi." Kasen awkwardly waves. The disapproving pair scoffs at him before moving on.

"Are you enjoying yourself?" Melony offers Kasen a handkerchief.

"Would you be offended if I said no?"

She chuckles. "Not what you're used to, but tonight was only made possible by the efforts of you and your friends. Lord Edwin is a man who truly wants to see Evenrise flourish."

"I guess I'm grateful for that." Kasen half-smiles. It seems to him, though, that Edwin is trying to take the credit without doing any work.

"Would you like to dance?" Melony doesn't wait for Kasen to answer. Taking his hand, she leads him to the dance floor.

Ashli, still isolated in the corner, watches Kasen's rhythmless motion and lack of coordination. But at the same time, she can't take her eyes off them. Melony only laughs at Kasen lack of experience before showing him how to move correctly. Soon enough, their movements synchronize.

"Lady Ashli." Edwin approaches her, and dismisses the ladies at his side. "Words can't describe how amazing you look tonight. Allow me the opportunity to express my gratitude for getting rid of those Feral marauders. A Ruler must care for ALL citizens, regardless of their origin."

Ashli responds as she often does: an irritated sigh or mumble, or not at all.

"We've to discuss your role in Evenrise's future," Edwin adds quietly. "You've become an icon among the people, including the Nobles. Your name alone has power. But this also puts a target on your back—both outside the city, and within. Those seeking to return Evenrise to its social stratification may take extreme measures to usurp you."

"Sounds like they're wasting their time," Ashli replies, but her focus lingers on Kasen and Melony. Edwin stands in her line of sight.

"My Lady. I can't stress the severity of this matter." Edwin's voice becomes stern. "Before your arrival, there were altercations about who truly deserves to be Evenrise's Ruler. You're no doubt the true successor, so we're expecting great things from you."

Ashli responds to Edwin's outcry with a dark and cold stare—all that is needed for him to back off. Edwin composes himself.

"I beg your forgiveness, My Lady. Things have grown stressful as of late. Pardon me." Edwin promptly leaves.

'How'd I get here?' Kika wonders from where she stands in the dark halls of Edwin's manor. *'Maybe after I close my eyes for a sec, I'll be with my companion again.'*

She does. And she opens them to see a hyena Bizarre in fine leathers staring pointblank back at her.

"Dammit. Guess I'll try again." Kika ignores the uncomfortably close stranger.

"Wait!" he yelps at her.

"Oh, hey. When did you get here?"

"Kika. It's me, Benji. Didn't your asshole of a father tell you about me?" As Kika ponders his question, Benji stares at her with a hooded gaze. "I can't believe how beautiful you've grown. You're even more beautiful than in my dreams. At last, we've united." Benji reaches his hand out to her.

"Lady Kika. What are you doing away from the banquet?" Wilbert's arrival disrupts Benji's advances. "If you'll follow me, Lord Edwin has an urgent message for you and your comrades."

"Another game? That sounds fun." Kika runs past him.

"Old man," Benji growls.

"Ill-mannered like the others." Wilbert leaves before his fit begins.

"Welcome, everyone." Edwin greets Kasen, Ashli, Kika along with the Fairest Council as they meet on the patio of his roof. "There's no better way of saying it: Even with Evenrise's massive social shift, we still lack the military might to engage in all-out war. Fairest Council and I met earlier today, and we've formulated a plan to not only strengthen our numbers, but also weaken theirs. Towns and villages many miles from Evenrise are willing to align themselves against the Feral menace. Among them are several experienced soldiers and military strategists.

We've sent trained soldiers to secure these locations, until the real battle commences."

"You three will be undergoing a very critical assignment," Gyra tells Kasen, Ashli, and Kika. "Edwin's made contact with a sanctuary village located near the Southerland coast. This particular village shelters human refugees."

"And you sure about this information, Edwin?" Omar asks. "There haven't been any records of human activity for nearly a decade."

"I didn't believe it at first, either, Commander, but Tauro—the village caretaker—has more knowledge about the Feral than most. You three and a selected team will be working alongside him and his apprentices."

Wilbert hands them four separate documents of hand-drawn Apparitions. Tauro is a tall ox Bizarre. The other three—Morris, a lean and dark Norm; Daphne, a Normish hare; and Gunter, a boar Bizarre— were friends from the Slum District that had escaped several years ago. Kasen is quietly flabbergasted. He can't believe this is where they've gone, and that he'd be seeing them again.

"Keeping this village secure is our top priority, so I highly recommend you get some rest before departing. You'll journey out two days from now. That'll be all for tonight."

As everyone leaves, Edwin calls Kasen back by name.

"May I have a quick word?" He waits for the others to mill out. "I finally get the opportunity to meet you. Your courage and dedication have inspired many. I can't imagine the hardships you've endured."

"I don't think anyone who spends their time feasting and drinking from atop their palace could," Kasen dares.

"That was a bit harsh, don't you think? But there's no wrong in your statement, either. You've every reason to hold a grudge against those more fortunate. I thought to take this time for us to reconcile. War approaches, and when our enemies come, it won't matter where we're from or who has had the better turnout in life. The social laws that divided Evenrise and caused such grief to many were established before I took my father's place. I'm only asking that you judge my actions for what they are now. Though I commend your efforts to free your district, I can't abide by any actions that'll put this city and its citizens at risk. Even if the laws aren't fair, they're the least disruptive solution."

"I think I understand."

"Smart boy," Edwin grants him. "Despite all, I'm intrigued to know how you became acquainted with the Sacred Born."

"Mostly coincidence," Kasen admits. "I'm not entirely sure how to explain it."

"I'll accept that," says Edwin. "Her role as Ruler over Evenrise has more weight than this battle. If she becomes distracted by any means, I'll personally do what I must to remove the problem."

Kasen fidgets awkwardly. He isn't quite sure what to say.

"Hm. Go get your rest. You'll need to be at peak condition for this assignment.

"Kasen. Wake up!" Vonnie shakes him.

"Vonnie? What time is it?" Kasen yawns.

"It's Lars, he's leaving." Jumping out of bed, Kasen and Vonnie scurry to the main entrance of Evenrise. A moderately sized army is already gathered there, saying their goodbyes to friends and family. Leading the army stands Omar, Vincent, Jaq, and Sloth.

"Hey, kid, you're just in time to say goodbye." Lars has donned the new Academy uniform.

"Where are you going?" Kasen asks.

"That's classified," Omar growls. "Don't you have your own thing to worry about, Slum boy?"

"He wants a goodbye kiss from his crush," snaps Jaq.

"Listen, kids. It's not smart thinking that everything will turn out the way you want. Especially in warfare. We all have roles to play. Until we come back, your orders are to make sure Evenrise remains standing. You've grown to be one tough S.O.B., kid." He gives Kasen a pat on the shoulder. "From here on, the choices you make will affect everyone. Make me proud."

"We're moving out," Omar barks. The main gates of Evenrise open. Lars gives Kasen one last friendly pat before he departs with the others.

"Are you OK, Kasen?" Vonnie asks, seeing his blank expression.

"Kika, Ashli, and I are being sent south. I don't know how long we'll be gone for," he says.

"I see." Vonnie's bummed look eventually turns back into a smile. "No worries. I'll fill your position till you come back. You will come back?"

"Of course," Kasen assures her. As the main gate closes, Kasen promises Lars he'll work as hard as he can to keep Evenrise safe.

VILLAGE OF HARMONY

Kasen, Ashli, Kika, and the selected United Apparition Soldiers journey to the Southerlands, a subtropical region of gulls, iguanas, and crabs.

The Village Harmony has long been safely hidden under lush palm forest. Beyond the forest lay the sands of the coast and murky brown sea. Apparitions believed nothing existed beyond it. Thus it was named: Sea of Naught, or Naught Sea.

The militia nears their destination. Here, Kasen will reunite with long lost fellows.

"Hey, Ash, you never told me what type of guys our companion's into," Kika whispers to her.

"This again?" She flashes a dull look.

Just then, however—interrupting their chatter—Kasen tells his new fellows the story he's kept to himself all these years.

"So... you DO have other friends," Kika coos in surprise the moment he's finished.

'What crisis will he put himself in this time?' Ashli thinks.

Patrolmen appear from the thick shrubs and trees. They wear leather uniforms with clasped hands stitched over the chest—Harmony's insignia. Their spears teem at the ready.

"Who goes there?"

"Maybe he's into guys in uniforms," Kika nudges Ashli.

An Elite soldier hands the patrolman a scroll with Tauro's signature. "The United Apparitions have been requested by your leader."

The patrolmen murmur to each other. They seem not to have received word of outside assistance.

"It's OK; I'll take it from here!" Daphne, the Normish hare—lineage made apparent by the rabbit ears attached to her head and her bunnyish nose—squeezes through the Harmony patrolmen, and wastes no time expressing her joy to see Kasen.

"I never thought I'd see you again," she cries, relieved to gaze upon him. "You've really grown. When did you become a soldier?"

"A lot's changed since the last time you saw me," Kasen happily tells her.

Daphne escorts the United Apparition Soldiers through Harmony. It's a small community of huts and tents. Village guards have been positioned both on the ground and on balconies built in the trees. Apparition villagers are busy with their day-to-day chores. The humans camp separately from them.

"It's not much, but at least it's not the Slum District," Daphne says. "We've already set up where your team will be posted during your time here."

"Little man, how you been?" A boar Bizarre puts Kasen in a friendly headlock.

"Gunter?! You've gotten… big." Kasen pulls himself free.

"It's mostly fat." He slaps his gut.

"Maybe he's into big guys." Kika nudges Ashli again. She rolls her eyes.

"It's hard believing you're an actual soldier now," Gunter commends.

"It is true you're harboring human refugees?" Kasen asks.

"That's mostly overseen by Morris and Tauro," replies Daphne.

"And the humans aren't too thrilled about being here, either," says Gunter. "You know, with all that happened between them and Apparitions."

"Speaking of which. Where is Morris?" When Kasen asks, Daphne and Gunter stare sternly at one another.

"About him. You see…"

"Nothing, because you have no self-awareness." It was the dark Norm, Morris. Between the three, Morris had clearly undergone the most change. He's taller and more slender than when Kasen last saw him.

"Ashli. Maybe he's into black—" Ashli presses her finger over Kika's lips.

"Tauro wants to speak with you three." Morris indicates Kasen, Ashli, and Kika. "Daphne, Gunter. Take the others to their post."

Kasen was hoping to speak with Morris, but unlike Daphne and Gunter, Morris doesn't seem as thrilled to see him again. The walk to Tauro's tipi is a silent one. Incense fills their nostrils as they enter. Tauro, the ox Bizarre, had been engaged in reading literature from an earlier Era. His gown consists of multilayered robes.

"Welcome to the Village of Harmony." Tuaro closes his novel and rises to meet them. "Edwin has spoken highly of you three, and I was eager to see for myself. Your documents have described much to us, so I'll skip the introduction. I created Harmony as a starting point to reform a long-lost alliance between humans and Apparitions. I'm thankful to receive Evenrise's assistance as the Feral threat worsens."

"Thank you for giving us the opportunity," Kasen replies graciously.

"We're not entirely sure why so many Feral have migrated so far from their homes in the Uncharted Territories. But their growing presence has caused tensions to rise within the village for some time."

"I still don't think we need Legion's assistance," Morris grunts. "We've been doing fine without them." Everyone looks to him in the wake of his sharp remark. He shows no signs of apologizing, so Tauro does for him.

"Excuse him. He wasn't entirely thrilled when I told him that we'd be having additional help. You are Kasen?" Tauro turns to address him. "Morris has informed me you also lived in Evenrise's Slum District? I can't imagine living in such an awful place."

"And that it's also in the past. No point in agonizing over it," Morris says, leaving Kasen astonished.

"Agonizing? How can you say something like that?" he squawks.

"You don't look like you're agonizing in that uniform," Morris snaps back.

"Aaaaand...kiss," says Kika.

One of Tauro's men barges in. "We've intercepted Feral off the coast."

"Again?" shrieks Tauro.

"They never learn. I'll take care of them," Morris promises.

"We'll help," offers Kasen. "It's why we're here in the first place."

"Fine. But I won't be taking orders from Legion."

FOREVER WILL END

The clash between Harmony Soldiers and Feral had already begun. The panic of impending battle peals throughout the village as its residents prepare to evacuate in case the Feral break through the defenses.

"Hopefully Legion's capable of squaring up against a measly Feral squad," Morris says as he and several more Harmony soldiers charge ahead into the battlefield.

"You have strange friends," Ashli comments before she, too, goes to battle, followed by fellow United Apparition soldiers.

"What are you waiting for? Go to him!" Kika ushers, and Kasen proceeds into battle with the others. She wipes away a happy tear. "It's so beautiful."

Kasen loses track of Ashli and Morris in the mayhem. Both enemy and ally fall as he weaves through the clashing of swords and thrusting of spears. He comes upon a heavy Feral that has gouged the eyes of a United Apparition solider. His sadistic gaze chooses Kasen as its next victim. The Feral shoves his way past the minor skirmishes happening around him. Pulling out a serrated machete, plunging into a berserk state, he violently swings at Kasen.

His blows are too slow and predictable to land a hit, but they cut down anyone unfortunate enough to get in the way. Swinging downward, the Feral's machete wedges itself in the mud and sand. As he angrily tries pulling it free, Kasen takes advantage of the opening and plunges his black sword into the Feral's abdomen.

Painful screams turn to laughter, and he throws Kasen to the ground. The Feral yanks the black blade from his middle and tosses it aside. Kasen scurries for his sword, but the Feral kicks him over and plants a massive foot upon his chest. The Feral laughs as Kasen struggles to lift it.

A mace crushing into the back of the skull sends the Feral toppling over. It is Morris who has saved him, and with a weapon that gives Kasen chills.

"Why are you carrying that?" Kasen demands.

"Because I don't forgive," Morris says, pulling the mace out of the Feral's head.

When the Feral numbers dwindle, they scurry back into the woods. The bodies litter the shore and paint the sands crimson.

Though battle had been won, it didn't bring calm to the villagers—especially not the human refugees.

"Please, if everyone will calm down, we can settle this problem." Back in Harmony, Daphne and Gunter try to lower the tension among their neighbors.

"We didn't ask for your help, Apparitions. Nor do we want it." It's Eugene—a stocky middle-aged man who often speaks for the humans.

"It's too dangerous with Feral lurking around," Gunter counters.

"You Apparitions are nothing but dangerous," snaps Heather, Eugene's only daughter. At eighteen years, she is his only remaining family.

"What's going on here?" Tauro intervenes. The victorious soldiers arrive moments after.

"We see past what you claim this place to be. When you all die, your graves will be pissed on until your tombs decay to rubble," Heather shrieks. Her father pulls her back.

"Refugees and guests. We understand how your stressful situation is, but wandering unfamiliar lands isn't practical for the time being. We promise that when the Feral are no longer a threat, you'll be free to go wherever you please."

"When will that be?" Eugene expects an answer. "Tomorrow? Next week? Ten years from now? We humans don't rely on your precious Aura to survive. Each day your men grow fewer, and your resources dwindle."

"That's why we've come to help," Kasen assures them, marked by battle, entering the crowd.

Heather sneers. "Who the hell are you?"

"We're the United Apparitions. The army sent here from Evenrise."

The humans laugh. "A real Apparition military? Are you fucking kidding me?"

Morris points his mace at Heather, intensifying the situation. "Why are you humans being so stubborn?"

"Take your toy off my daughter, Apparition." Eugene warns.

"Or what? You're going to hound me about being an Apparition some more? Go on, old man, do your worst."

"Morris, what are you doing?" Kasen puts himself in between the mace and Heather.

"They're not listening. Why would they rather be brutally murdered by Feral than receive our protection?"

"Put that away," Kasen insists. "They're already frightened; you're making it worse."

"So do you what you came here to do and fix it, Legion." Morris angrily turns to leave.

"What's your problem? You're acting like I did something wrong. You don't care about the Slum District, and now you're scaring already frightened people? What would Celia think if she saw you acting this way?"

Enraged by the sound of that name, Morris tackles tackles Kasen to the ground. Everyone watches as the two roll across the dirt, fighting the way two angry boys would.

"See? I told you," Kika nudges Ashli once more.

Morris gains the edge over Kasen. Pinning him on his back, he grabs his mace, and brings it down near Kasen's head. Only intense panting fills the silence.

"That's enough, you two," Tauro shouts. "Morris, come with me now."

"Ever mention her again, I'll bash your face in," Morris warns Kasen, his expression dark and steaming. But he gets off of him, and follows Tauro.

"I think we've had our fill of Apparitions for today." Eugene and the other humans return to their tents.

Daphne and Gunter help Kasen off the ground. His cheek and eye are already swelling, and sting at the slightest touch. Drops of blood fall from his nose. His face, arms, and legs are covered with scratches and bruises.

Gunter looks a little guilty. "We wanted to tell you Morris hasn't been himself after everything that's happened."

"We hoped he would've cheered up a little after seeing you," Daphne adds.

"You're right," Kasen manages, leaning over to push out a line of red spit. "He's changed a lot."

As the sun sets on Harmony, the stars come into view. Kasen takes his patrol station on the balconies over the village, where he listens to the sounds of the ocean. He realizes he hasn't had a night this peaceful since he and Vonnie climbed their old tree in the Slum District. Things have changed a lot for him in only a year's time.

"What now?" Ashli spies Kasen slumped over a balcony rail.

"Do you dwell on the past?" he asks. "Is there anything too important that you can't let go, or maybe something that made you into the person you are today? I knew Morris wasn't ever a fan of Legion—I mean, the United Apparitions. I wasn't sure what he'd think once he knew I joined them. I still wonder if joining Legion was the right thing to do, or if I was just being selfish."

Ashli pages back to a certain memory. It was not merely the pain of being humiliated by her mother time and time again; it was a darker memory that became the seed for her quest to achieve great power.

She shuts this memory out, hiding any sign of vulnerability. "Dwelling on the past is for those too weak to focus on what's happening now. What's done is done. That's all there is to it."

"Pretty much the response I expected." Kasen chuckles. "But thanks for answering, anyways. It's not like you to usually care enough to respond."

Ashli turns away from him. She'd never been flattered before.

"You almost let your anger get the better of you, Morris." Tauro watches as his soldier quickly paces back and forth.

"Why did you bring him here? He shouldn't have come," Morris seethes. "Bringing Legion here at all was a mistake. They ruin everything."

"I thought you'd be happy to see your long-lost friend among the Elite troops. Would you rather he be begging for scraps in a broken alley?"

"I wouldn't wish that on anyone." The truth of his own words calms Morris some. "I thought after everything that happened, he'd steer clear of that place, and those people. He seemed so proud to wear the uniform."

"Remember the day I found you?" Tauro calmly circles him. "You were an angry, distraught lad. You didn't get along well with the others. Even Daphne and Gunter had shunned you. But I saw what they couldn't. All that anger and bitterness you harbor is a power waiting to be unleashed upon your enemies. Your friend Kasen is the last obstacle that prevents you from digging deeper into your potential."

"He's my friend. Why would he be an obstacle?"

"He chose Legion over you. The same Legion that has brought you many years of grief. If you told him of your ambitions, do you think he'd stand with or against you?"

"Of course he'd stand with me? If he's truly my friend, he will." Morris is certain of this—though perhaps not quite so certain of Kasen's loyalties.

"And if he chose to stand against you?" Tauro wonders sternly.

"I'm doing this for Celia. Either way, he won't be an obstacle."

"I only pray—for his sake—he won't. You've had a long day, Morris. Go and rest."

"Thank you, Tauro." Morris bows before exiting his tipi.

With Morris gone, Tauro reaches under his bed and pulls out a small chest. It contains an ancient black book with a red hand glowing on the center.

"Poor, demented Morris. A minor chord in my symphony of conquest. My prayers will be answered. Brother Garrick, I thank you for your sacrifice. The troops of Evenrise are scattered from the city. The daughter of the Devil traitor, Malik, is within my grasp. With the Gospel of Chaos in my possession, my claim to rule all is assured."

UNKINDLED FRIENDSHIP

On a moonless night, worn by Tauro's lies and the constant threat of Feral invasion, the humans reach their limit. They carry out a plan to escape.

"Dad? What are you doing?" Heather wakes to find her father and others dragging Harmony guards into their tent. "Did you—?"

"They'll be awake soon. There's no time to waste." The guards are stripped bare. "We're getting you out of here tonight."

"What about you?" Eugene doesn't answer, concentrating on the task at hand. "Dad. I'm not going anywhere without you."

"We need to get moving," sharply whispers the lookout.

Eugene gives Heather the guard's garments. "I'm not losing my remaining family to those Apparition fiends. You've heard us talking about the militia of humans searching for lost and captured refugees. Few of us are in any sort of condition to wander the wilderness. But we can hold Tauro and his goons off long enough for you get clear away from here. And even if you're unable to find them, you must live on for me. Please."

Heather heeds her father, and changes into the guard's uniform. The lookout takes her hand without leaving them enough time to say a real goodbye.

Posing as patrol men, they exchange wordless pleasantries with those they pass by, strolling to a meeting place where they join a small group of other able-bodied humans. Once the coast is clear, they swiftly escape deep into the woods.

FOREVER WILL END

All seems normal as the sun rises over the village several hours later. The residents busy themselves with their usual daily tasks.

"It's like old times, but better, you know." Daphne works with Kasen and Gunter on their daily schedule. "This is how it was in the Slum District. Us taking care of the unfortunate."

"Only this time Legion's not trying to kill any of us...no offense," Gunter says to Kasen.

"You're right," Kasen replies. "If only things had changed sooner, maybe Celia would be—" A series of bells ringing throughout the village cuts him off.

"What's going on?" he asks.

Daphne and Gunter exchange worried looks. "Someone's missing..."

"How'd humans manage to jump you?" Tauro scolds the guards who came-to moments ago. They're still stripped bare. "Which humans are missing?!"

As if Tauro needed to ask. He pushes the guards out of his way and marches over to Eugene's tent, barging inside.

"Where have they gone?"

"Who?" Eugene sounds surprised.

"The humans who assaulted my men, took their uniforms, and ran away," Tauro shrieks.

"What reason would they have to do that? This village is safe. Or you've done well convincing us it is."

"Why must you humans remain hostile?" Tauro's agitation heightens. "I've only provided you with my hospitality."

"I'm still here," Eugene offers as proof of his words.

Morris joins the dispute. He enters the tent with a quick and confident stride. "We know you had something to do with their escape. You're not very smart to send away your only daughter. Especially with Feral roaming the woods."

"I won't debate with Tauro's lackey. If you're not OK with us leaving when we choose, then that makes us prisoners, not guests."

"So that's what you think? Alright, listen up, humans." Morris shouts to get their attention. "Anyone who feels they're here against their will is free to go, because apparently our protection's too generous. We won't stop you, but whatever lurks beyond the village will." When the humans refuse to respond to his outburst, he scoffs away.

"I hope you're satisfied. Whatever happens to them's on you, Eugene." Tauro makes his leave, as well.

Eugene angrily squats on his bed and rubs his head in frustration.

"Excuse me. Eugene, sir." Kasen enters his home.

"Don't you Apparitions know how to knock before you enter?" he grumbles.

"With your permission. The United Apparitions would like to search for your daughter and the others who escaped or fled."

"Did they escape, or flee?" Eugene asks. "There's a difference, boy."

"I—uh. The United Apparitions were tasked to protect the people of Harmony. If there's a any way we can help you..."

Eugene angrily shoots from his bed. "You think you're 'helping' us after your kind have nearly wiped out humanity? You help out of pity. Would you act as kindly if I tortured, raped, and murdered those you love right before your eyes? You can pretend to act different from those Feral—you'll burn in hell just as quickly. My daughter's safe, and that's all I care about. Now get the hell out."

Kasen swallows the lump stuck in his throat. "We'll make sure your daughter and the others are safe; if they return, it'll be because they chose to. I'm sorry, sir."

He quickly exits Eugene's tent, rejoining his fellow soldiers.

"Go and look for the missing humans? On whose authority?" Tauro questions the United Apparitions soldiers as they prepare a search party.

"Our orders were to keep this village and its residents safe."

"And I was given complete authority over your team. I can't afford to dispatch a search party when Feral could attack at any moment."

"Kasen. This is a waste of time," Morris tells Kasen as he helps the squadron prepare. "They snuck out in the middle of the night. They've almost half a day on you and there's hardly a trail. They obviously don't want to be found."

"The Morris I remember would've searched the moment he found out they went missing, and wouldn't have returned until they were found, no matter how long it took. It's the right thing to do, or did you forget that, too?"

"Obnoxious little fuck," Tauro grits through his teeth as the search party picks up its kit and stalks for the forest.

"Companion, where are you going?" Kika hangs upside down in a tree.

"Looking for the humans. Can't play right now," Kasen says, and the search team hurries along.

"But companion, you're...going the wrong way." Her warning comes too late for them to hear. "Oh, well. I'm better at this game, anyways." Kika drops down and playfully ventures on her own into the woods.

"That disrespectful bastard. He'll ruin everything." Once the soldiers disappear into the palms, it's Tauro's turn to angrily pace back and forth. "I should've let you finish that fight, Morris."

"Tauro. Kasen's only trying to..."

"NO MORE DEFENDING HIM, MORRIS!" Tauro's bellow spooks him. "He's the same as the other Legion scum who've ruined your life. There's no doubt in my mind that he'll stop you from taking vengeance for Celia's death. The plan will move forward sooner than anticipated. You'll overcome your obstacle tonight."

"I will," Morris agrees, but there is hesitation in his voice that wasn't there before.

As Kasen and the team search for the missing humans, the memory of Eugene scolding him still weighs heavily on his mind.

'I'm sorry we Apparitions have cause you and many humans to suffer as you have,' he thinks, trudging through the tangled jungle undergrowth. *'If you took everything I cherished, I'd wish the worst for you, too. But I'd forgive you, because I'd rather allow myself to be free of that pain than have it consume me. I hope someday you'll allow yourself to do the same.'*

An arrow intended for him misses and sinks into the back of a soldier beside him. Feral emerge from behind and above the trees. The United Apparitions clash with their ambushers.

The clash ends quickly. Having accomplished their goal of slowing the search party, the Feral retreat deeper into the forest, leaving many

United Apparition soldiers injured. The search is suspended, and those still able-bodied carried the wounded back to Harmony for treatment.

In Harmony, Daphne and Gunter spy Morris walking alone. They call to him, but are ignored. They quickly catch up.

"Morris? You look terrible, man," Gunter remarks on his cold exterior.

"It's getting late. We're worried about Kasen and the others," Daphne says.

"Why do you guys suddenly care about him so much?" Morris demands. "Ever since he arrived, you won't shut up about him. He abandoned us, and now he stands with the enemy."

"Morris, you're scaring us." Daphne is careful to speak softly. "Since we showed up here, you've been acting different. We try talking to you, but for some reason, you're always... angry."

"How angry!" Morris sharply snaps at her. "Was it from those Higher Up assholes harassing us every damn day, or was it Celia, who Legion discarded like trash—the same people she looked to as parents. Which is it?"

"She was a kind woman, Morris. She taught us to do the right thing," Gunter murmurs. "Why aren't you honoring her?"

Morris clutches Gunter by his neck and pins him against a nearby tree.

"Morris, let him go!" cries Daphne, and she tries pulling him off. She's pushed to the ground.

"The right thing is to dismantle Legion the way they dismantled Celia," Morris, fuming, insists. "They couldn't have prayed for a better soldier, but instead of helping her in her time of need, they killed her... they killed my mother like she was nothing." He releases his hold on Gunter. "Since Kasen has sided with the enemy, he'll be destroyed with them."

Morris departs from a fearful Daphne and Gunter. They can only watch him go.

As evening creeps into the Southerlands, the humans who escaped the night prior gather around their small fire. The unsettling noises of wildlife howl and hoot all around them. Having only each other for comfort, they ration what they can.

"Leaving was a mistake," one says.

"Let's go back," suggests another.

"Do you remember the way?"

"We're lost. How are we supposed to find some specialist team in the middle of the woods?"

"Everyone listen to me," Heather says. "That village was dangerous. We can't trust Apparitions now or ever. It's better this way. Besides, we've nearly a day on them. They won't find us out here."

"Found you!" Kika's appearance scares the humans half-to-death. "That was easy. You guys suck at hiding... but so does my companion."

"I know you." Heather recognizes her. You're that weird Apparition. You're alone?"

"No. For the last time, my name's Kika," she insists.

"I meant ARE you alone?" Heather asks, impatient, again.

"Oh... also no."

"But you're the only Apparition here. And we're far from the village. How'd you find us so quickly?"

"Well, I already said you suck at hiding. And I was alone. Until these guys started following me." Feral appear from the dark brush and surround Kika and the humans. "I think they want to play, too. I never asked..."

Eugene washes his face and arms at the communal well pump. He sees Ashli watching him.

"What are you staring at, Apparition."

"You're no ordinary human. You harness Aura. The power channeled only by Apparitions."

"Your point?"

"You possess the strength to obtain the freedom you sought after this whole time, yet you remain imprisoned."

"Some Apparitions were kind enough to teach humans how to conjure Aura. I needed to protect my family. It was a short-term alliance that I've regretted. Having great power isn't what it's cracked up to be, and many—including myself—found out the hard way. Now, are we done here, or do you want to watch me bathe?"

"You've only explained how much of a failure you are." Ashli's remark makes Eugene more attentive. "That boy who's searching for your child has failed a plethora of times. The only difference is that he realizes it, and through some miracle, manages to exceed everyone's expectations. You blame everyone but yourself. If your daughter's taken by Feral, they won't kill her, they'll reduce her into another reminder of the failure you've become."

Eugene lightly chuckles at Ashli's harsh words. "Why can't Tauro be this honest?"

"Why would you expect honesty from a Feral...?"

"Kasen. Oh my goodness." Daphne hurries to him as he and the search party carry their wounded into the village. Daphne and Gunter assist.

"An ambush," Kasen informs them. "It was as if they expected us. He lets out an uncomfortable grunt when Daphne rubs alcohol over the cut on his arm. "I'll be fine, please tend to the others."

"You got it," Gunter says, carrying an injured soldier over his back to the infirmary. Daphne goes with him.

Eugene approaches Kasen. "Your search party's been out all day."

"We couldn't find anything," he regrets, sincere, "but we'll keep looking."

"I'm grateful that you were willing to risk your lives to find them, despite my cruelty from before."

Kasen's startled by the unexpected gratitude. "Th—thank you, sir."

"Couldn't find them?" Morris joins their conversation.

"I'll continue searching after a moment. Where's Tauro?" wonders Kasen.

"He's out running an errand, and left me in charge. I was just informed by some guards that there's fresh footprints off the coast. I'm gonna go check it out."

"I'll join you, if that's OK," Kasen half-asks, half-tells.

"Suppose I've nothing better to do, either," says Ashli.

"I'll join, as well." Eugene steps up. "If they only see Apparitions, they'll scurry."

"Alright, then. Let's get going."

As the four journey to the coast, Eugene and Ashli keep their eyes trained on Morris while he and Kasen converse.

"When I heard you joined Legion, I was skeptical. I thought you might've forgotten everything that happened before."

"I'd never forget," Kasen swears. "People were dying, and it needed to stop. I didn't think it'd turn out like this."

"And you're OK with the choices you've made?" Morris asks.

"The Slum District's no more. If I had to do it all over, I wouldn't change anything."

"I see." Morris's reply is cold.

Arriving at the coast, Kasen immediately looks for clues or footprints in the sand, but finds nothing. Despite the many battles fought here, it's mesmerizing under the moon and stars.

"Why would they come to the coast?" Kasen asks. "They'd be spotted in no time at all."

"Because I didn't send my daughter and the others this way." Eugene turns to Morris. "This is where you plan to do it?"

"At least it's pleasant scenery," he figures.

"Scenery? For what?" Kasen asks.

"Can you not tell friend from assassin?" dares Ashli.

"Assassin? Morris?" Kasen turns to him. Sees the bitterness written across his face.

"You've sided with the enemy." Morris draws his mace.

"Where's my daughter and the others?" Eugene growls.

"I honestly don't care." Morris's doesn't take his eyes off Kasen. "You honestly thought I'd be thrilled to see you've become Legion's newest goon? Tauro was right when he said you've turned your back against your true friends."

"Eugene. Ashli. Get the villagers out of Harmony. I'll talk to Morris alone," Kasen says.

"You can't win," Ashli bluntly replies.

"Please, Ashli. If I've ever asked you for anything, it's now. Please don't let anything happen to them."

"Let's go, Apparition." Eugene says. After a moment of hesitation, Ashli follows.

"It just us now, Morris. Tauro's been screwing with your head. You never acted like this until you met him."

"You're slow to catch on. The Legion's atrocities can't be forgiven."

Kasen tries reasoning with him. "They've changed, Morris. They're working hard to right their wrongs."

"So that makes everything OK? I was powerless to save Celia then, but thanks to Tauro, I'm strong enough to avenge her. He told me you were the last obstacle for me to overcome. I understand what I have to do."

"This is what Celia was afraid of," argues Kasen. "You, acting out of anger. She fought to make the world a better place for everyone and taught us to do the same. If you go down this road, you'll only hurt people. I won't let you do that." The black sword appears in Kasen's hand.

Morris chuckles darkly. "Seems as though it was yesterday we scoured the Slum streets for anything we could find. We valued the lives of the sick and injured more than our own. Despite how shitty things were, I was happy and proud knowing I was helping others. Now I just guard selfish humans who don't show a damn bit of gratitude."

"You can still be that person, Morris."

"If you've chosen to fight in the name of Legion, you'll die in the name of Legion." Morris initiates their fight, launching a furry of swings that Kasen struggles to defend against. "I expected more from a Legion grunt. If you fail here, Legion's finished. Is that what you want?!"

"What I want is the Morris I remember back," Kasen yells as their weapons clash together.

"You lost him the moment you put on that uniform."

Kasen retaliates with a head-butt. Knocking Morris to the ground, and putting him in a daze.

"If that's true, then I'll do what I must to protect the people of Evenrise and Harmony." Kasen closes in on Morris, ready to land the fatal strike. "Forgive me, Celia."

A soft voice echoes in his head. Unexpectedly, the black sword vanishes. Kasen's left empty-handed, and defenseless, and dumbfound. A mace crushes into his chest, the impact enough to make Kasen vomit blood as he sails through the air, and rolls bodily across the coastal sands.

Morris follows the red trail to where Kasen lies, gargling. His uniform brightens with the stain of his fatal wound.

Kasen tries to speak, but can only choke.

"You're finished, Kasen. Even if it's not by my hand, Legion's destined to fall. I've proven that old friends won't stand in my way of vengeance. You may have thought you were doing the right thing, but your choices were wrong." Morris leaves Kasen where he lies.

Kasen can't move, speak, blood fills his lungs, and his vision darkens.

"Celia..." He musters his last words before darkness overtakes him. "I failed."

THE NOT TOO GOOD OLE DAYS/SIGIL OF CORRUPTION

A furious winter storm blisters through the city of Evenrise as the cold season begins.

In an alley that staves off the freezing winds, a younger boy wrapped inside a thick blanket awakens. He surveys unfamiliar surroundings. He's unsure how he came to be here.

Unwrapping himself, he feels the cold over his naked flesh, and quickly rewraps. There is a necklace around his neck with a latched medallion. Engraved on it, the name *Kasen*.

He leaves the alleys, fighting the blizzard into open streets. There, others cluster together to keep warm, their old and ragged clothing providing little protection. They fight each other over small fires, desperate for their turn to thaw. Those who succumb to the cold are stripped of their clothes and piled. Some of the corpses miss limbs, and often, a foul stench wafts from the Slum fires.

He quickly moves past them, and accidently bumps into a heavier man.

"Damn kids," the man growls as he tries grabbing Kasen's blanket. Kasen runs from him.

He keeps running, not sure where he is going, until he comes to a tall thorn fence. Wherever he is, getting out won't be easy. Perhaps it's not even possible.

"What's wrong, little guy?" says a soldier standing on the other side. "You wanna get out, don't you? I'll tell ya how, but ya have to keep it a secret."

FOREVER WILL END

Kasen presses against the fence so the soldier can whisper to him.

"You can get out after you go fuck yourself!" the soldier shouts in Kasen's ear. They laugh as they rattle the fence. "You should see your face, Slum boy."

Frightened of the soldiers, Kasen flees once more. He can hear their taunts cackle through the blizzard winds. Too distracted to see a foot sticking out to trip him, he face-plants into the snow.

"Lost, kid?" Two young hoodlums stand over Kasen. "You gotta pay to use this road. That blanket of yours should cover a bit."

Getting to his feet, Kasen steps away from them. A third youth appears behind him to shove Kasen forward; the first two strike him to the ground. They rip the blanket from him. Now Kasen lies bare in snow.

"Thanks, asshole." The leader of the trio wraps up in their newly acquired blanket. "This damn blizzard. When was the last time we ate good?"

"What about him? He looks filling," the second suggests.

"He's nothing but bones," says the third. "What about that fat cranky guy?"

"We already put in the work for this one; let's finish the job." The three hoodlums gather around the cold-numb Kasen and repeatedly kick him until his face goes bloody. "Tough shit to be him. Get the hatchet."

The leader shoves the second to fetch it. While doing so, they see that someone has been watching them. It's too hard to make out their appearance in the whirling snowflakes.

"Who's that?"

The leader gives a signal. "Look like the main course."

As the hoodlums attack the stranger, young Kasen slowly loses consciousness in the snow.

The Feral who captured Kika and the humans are cuffed in shackles, placed on boats, and sailed to a distant island fortress off the coast.

A sinister black cloud looms over the island. Even the Feral stir with fear the closer they come. Tauro awaits them on the beach.

"I knew that scumbag was up to no good," Heather spits.

"Like what?" Kika wonders, ever under the assumption this is all part of the game.

"Look where they're taking us. Just like we've always said about Apparitions. You're all savages."

"Quiet, human." A Feral yanks Heather's shackles. Once they reach land, the humans are removed from their cages.

"Let's hurry this up, Tauro," says the Feral, dragging Heather and the others along. "This place freaks us out and you know we're not welcome here."

"That'll change now that we have humans to sell. As well as you, Devil girl." Tauro smirks at the frightened humans.

The Feral slavers take the humans to a towering fortress made mostly of wood totems and rusted steel. At its entrance stand fierce men, most of their bodies dressed in tattoos, their weapons designed to tear flesh from bone.

"Tauro, is that you?" A guard prevents them from proceeding any further. "Who said you and your faithless lackeys could return?"

"If you got something to say," postures one of Tauro's men, spoiling for a fight, "say it to our faces."

"You all merely pretend to be faithful subjects, but when it comes to discipline, you Feral scum are the biggest cowardly shits I've ever met. Be thankful we haven't gone out of our way to kill the lot of you."

"Call us 'Feral' again." Tauro's men draw their weapons. Tauro has them sheath.

"We assure you our faith's as strong as yours," Tauro replies. "Today's Benji's birthday and we've brought him humans in show of good faith."

"Humans, huh?" The guard looks at Tauro in judgment. Then at the human captives. "Don't do anything stupid, Feral." He gives the go-ahead, and the gates of the fortress open to them.

"By Evil's Will." The guard salutes.

"By Evil's Will." Tauro humbly says back, before he and his men take the humans inside the fortress.

FOREVER WILL END

Something hitting against the side of a house wakes younger Kasen. He stirs in a strange bed, warmed by the glow of a small fire. On the floor next to him waits a set of folded clothes.

They're a bit big, but at least he isn't nude anymore. The beating the hoodlums gave him has been treated to some degree. Again, something hits against the side of the house.

Out of bed and changed, Kasen opens the door to the outside. The blizzard had died down sometime during his slumber. One more bang against the house.

Looking above him, Kasen sees the three hoodlums hanging over the roof. One, still alive, is kicking weakly for warmth.

"H—Hey, kid," the hoodlum gasps. "Tell that psycho I'm sorry for almost roasting you. We were hungry, was all. Get me down from here. Please." An arrow shot into the hoodlum's back by a soldier silences them.

"You're in a lot of trouble, kid," the shooter says, taking Kasen by his arm and steering him to a deserted plaza where a mature rat Bizarre, a boar Bizarre boy, a Normish hare girl, and a tall young Norm man wait on their knees. Another soldier paces back and forth between them, flaunting a long mace over his shoulder.

Kasen is thrown between the rat Bizarre and the dark young man.

"What's wrong, hunny bunny?" the mace-carrying soldier says to the crying Normish hare.

"Please. We haven't done anything," she whimpers.

"Can Slums ever tell the truth?" The soldier moves on to the young boar Bizarre, who sobs just as much. "Damn, I didn't know these Slum bastards came with extra fat." He chuckles as the boy cries even harder, then moves on to the rat Bizarre.

"Do you know what day it is?"

"Tue—Tuesday?" The rat Bizarre squeaks.

"My birthday." The young soldier flaunts his mace again.

"Happy Birthday?"

"My parents got me this badass mace. It belonged to some Feral Warlord—"

"Hey, don't mean to hurry you up because it's cold as hell, but will you hurry it up? It's cold as hell," his comrades complain.

"Alright, already," the soldier yells back, then turns hungry eyes on his captives. "We are here to deliver due justice. You Slums have been declared guilty of criminal activity by the good people of Evenrise. Petty thievery, for example." The soldier pulls Kasen's necklace out of the rat Bizarre's pocket.

"That was given to me in exchange for a set of clothes," he protests.

"Wrong. It's mine." The soldier puts on the necklace and tosses the medallion piece.

"Y—You can't falsely accuse us of crimes," the rat Bizarre shrieks.

"You know what I hate most about you Slums?" The soldier circles behind him. "Is that you exist."

He smacks his mace into the back of the rat Bizarre's head. The children wail in horror as he twitches uncontrollably with part of his head caved-in. The soldiers laugh and cheer.

"Oh, man. Do you see how fucked up his skull is? DID YOU SEE IT?" The soldier roughly holds his mace out to Kasen. Streaks of blood splatter his face. "What's your name, Slum pest?"

He is too scared to speak. "Ka—Ka—Kay—"

"Ca—Ca—Can't hear you." The mockery makes his comrades laugh. "Let's keep this party going."

Just as he circles around Kasen, the young Norm kneeling beside him springs to his feet and fights for the mace.

Another soldier quickly rushes over to end it. When he does, however, the Norm shifts his momentum so the mace whips across his face.

The others shriek at the sight of their friend's mutilated face. The Norm uses their shock to stomp on the mace-wielding soldier's foot and is able to take control of the weapon. He strikes the soldier's knee. Stricken, their tormentor falls to the ground, crying for dear life.

"Slum bastards," roars a soldier as they descend upon the Norm to avenge their comrades. The young boy jukes and ducks under their attacks. One of them is struck in the pelvis; if the impact wasn't enough to take their life, the heart attack they suffer does.

"Damn worthless Slum," the last soldier standing curses. "You'll pay for this."

But not today. Outmaneuvered, he retreats, abandoning his downed comrades—and leaving the mace-stripped soldier with his shattered knee to his fate.

"You're dead," the soldier grits, sweat streaming into his eyes, barely able to speak. "Do you hear me? All of you are fucking dead!"

He's put down by the crush of his own mace.

"You alright?" The young Norm offers a hand to the stunned Kasen. "I'm Morris. You'll be safer if you come with us..."

Upon being taken inside the island fortress, the first thing the humans see is flesh.

A ceremonial orgy is underway. Both men and women battle and ravage each other. Non-participants gorge themselves on roasted meat, tattoo one another, forge weapons, or round up vicious animals (wolves the size of lions, flesh eating rhinos, fearsome winged beasts). These Apparitions had never adapted from the warmongering eras. Violence is their language; words like peace, prosperity, joy are blasphemies. They live to worship the Will of Evil, and bring forth the End of Days Era. Their banner and sigil: the withered Black Hand.

The young hyena Bizarre, Benji, and a middle-aged panther Normish (her panther traits consisting of paws for feet, furry hands, and a long tail) oversee the festivities on their throne chairs. As the panther keeps watch over the throng, Benji enjoys a servant girl fondling him on all fours.

"Benji, dear, we have guest," the former notices. Benji's moan rankles into a groan.

When he sees that Kika is among the guests, however, he becomes ecstatic. Jumping from his chair, he knocks over his servant girl and stands, naked.

"You don't know how happy I am to see you again... in chains? Why are you in chains? WHY IS SHE IN CHAINS?" As Benji takes his rage out on one of Tauro's men by strangling them to death, the festivities of the fortress fall silent; even the orgy pauses. Before he can unleash more anger, the panther caresses his shoulders to calm him.

"Benji, what have we discussed about your outbursts? Don't waste your energy on these faithless Feral."

"B—But I'm the chosen Ruler. I want what I was promised." Benji pouts the way a spoiled child would.

"It's your birthday. Just enjoy what you have until then."

He takes a few deep breaths. "If I find out you put a finger on her, you'll be fed your own scrotum." Then he tugs the chain of his servant. "I haven't finished, which means you haven't finished." She follows Benji on all fours to his chambers.

"Wonder who that was?" Kika ponders.

"Corrinne. You're still as beautiful as always." Tauro compliments the panther left behind. He's long been smitten with her.

"Tauro. I was still under the impression I'd never see you again." Corrinne regards him with no interest. "What do you want this time?"

"To start off on a good note, I've brought you and his Majesty Benji humans to use for your... festivities." He motions for his men to bring Heather forward.

"Humans?" This perks Corrinne's ear. She strums a finger across Heather's chest and cheek. "You're a pretty human girl. Can you talk?"

"Get fucked, Apparition."

"So tempting." Corinne inhales Heather's scent, then exhales. "I've dreamed of sharing my bed with a human woman."

Tauro draws the conversation back. "I've more, should you happen to run out."

"Are we getting them before or after you're beaten to death?"

Tauro and men are restrained by Sigil-bearers. Many are stabbed multiple times. They repeatedly strike Tauro's face.

"Corrinne, please," Tauro rasps through the pain.

"I don't like you, Tauro. Your face, your name. Every breath you take makes my skin crawl."

"I've brought something far valuable than humans," he cries, pointing quickly to Kika. "Malik's daughter."

"Hello." She casually waves at the panther on her dais.

"He had a child?" Corrinne signals the Sigil-bearers off Tauro.

"His only child has been living in Evenrise." Tauro prostrates himself. "I know how your men endlessly hunt for that traitor and his slut whore, Kiera. With his daughter as your captive, he'll have to crawl from whatever hole he's hiding in. Lady Corrinne. I've worked tirelessly to earn my way back into your Sigil. Even as we speak, my pawn, Morris, travels to Evenrise on an idiotic quest for vengeance. Now I've brought Malik's daughter to you. This is more service than even your most loyal subordinates. The Cult that formed the Sigil have long since disbanded and are powerless. Absolve me of my exile, and allow me to command your armies, so I may rid this world of the true faithless heathens."

"You really must be passionate if you're risking your life. How could I refuse now?" She permits him to live with no more decorum than this. With a final turn of her twist, the bearers take the humans away. "Let's get our human friends settled into their new homes."

"You honor me, Corrinne."

With the taste of his false words lingering on his tongue, Tauro maliciously grins. His true intentions: to have Corrinne, and the Ruler's throne.

Young Kasen becomes quickly acquainted with Morris, Daphne, and Gunter. They lead him through a more pleasant area of the Slum District, pointing out landmarks like tour guides.

"I'm assuming you've met the district's ruder residents," says Morris. "Some of us understand that it's easier if we help each other rather than fight amongst ourselves. This is as good as it gets around here. Those soldiers from before were probably Legion's newest recruits." He continues. "They build their reputations on harassing Slum residents. What they did to the trader—" Morris clenches his fist. "I won't let that happen to one of ours again."

They come to an old cottage. Inside the dark and dusty home, a sickly woman rests on her bed. Her smile is weak yet warm upon seeing them enter.

"I'm back," Morris calls. "This is Kasen. And Kasen, this is my mother, Celia."

"Pleasure to meet you, young man. I apologize for lacking the condition to welcome you properly."

Kasen isn't sure what to say. "It's alright."

Morris changes the rags over her forehead. Celia spies scratch marks on his arm.

"What happened?"

"Just a few scratches, is all," Morris lies, but Celia isn't so easily fooled.

"You've been fighting again, haven't you?"

"They killed one of ours. They would've killed us, too, if I hadn't acted. They've no right to bully us."

"You were taught better than to stoop to their level," Celia rebukes, but can't continue. She slips into a hacking fit.

"You need to rest. We'll be right outside if you need anything. C'mon, Kasen."

As Morris leaves the cottage, Celia looks at her son with concern. Kasen follows after.

"We're going to get through this." Heather tries to cheer her human companions as they sit in the dark cells below the island fortress.

"This is you and your father's fault," a neighbor scolds her. "You made us believe escaping was our best bet to survive, and now look where we are. Tauro may be a piece of shit, but at least he didn't have us leave our loved ones behind."

They shun Heather from the group. She finds a corner in which to isolate herself. She isn't going to see her father again. She never had the chance to say goodbye. Tears of anger and sadness stream down her face.

"Isn't this the most epic game of hide-n'-seek ever?" Kika taps her shoulder.

"Leave me alone." Heather cradles herself tighter. "I should've stayed with my dad. We'll die here. I know we will."

"Oh… OK. Bye," she says, and retreats to the cell door. Heather and the other humans watch her curiously.

"What are you doing?"

A lone Sigil guard patrols the fortress cells. Judging from the leer on their face, they intend to have some pleasurable alone time with the human prisoners. But as they shuffle through a set of keys, they hear someone counting from within the cell block.

"Nine hundred ninety-eight. Nine hundred ninety-nine. One thousand! Ready or not, here I come!" Kika hits the cell door hard enough, it breaks off and crushes the Sigil guard into the wall. She happily skips and hums down the prison lane.

"We should probably follow her," Heather suggests, and for once, the humans unanimously agree.

"I appreciate your help, young man," Celia says as Kasen sweeps the floors of the cottage. "It's nice seeing Morris making friends. Things haven't been well for him the past few years. I'm thankful he'll have someone else turn to now."

All those years ago, Kasen hadn't fully understood what those words meant.

The cottage door bursts open, and without permission enters a woman, followed by two identical men. The woman runs her fingers across the wall, disgusted by the dust. One of the boys does the same, and playfully wipes it on the others nose. They giggle simultaneously, and become engaged in a dust-smearing game.

"What do you want, Chantel?' Celia's question is sharp.

"Celia," she coos, but her sympathy is as artificial as her manners. "My heavens, you look awful."

Celia wrestles down a violent cough. "It's no concern of yours."

"Of course it is. My duty to make sure the residents of the Slum District are cared for."

"By turning them into thieves and other ill-mannered people. Keep your treachery away from my son."

"What are YOU doing here?" Morris, accompanied by Daphne and Gunter, enters. He heads right for Celia's side.

"We were just talking about you," Chantel informs him. "I'm here because we're all trying provide care to our fellow Slum residents. Can't we just put the issues between us aside and work together?"

"Forget it," Morris snaps. "You and your two loverboys get out."

"Loverboys? What's he talking about, Yuan?"

"Haven't the slightest clue, Juan. Perhaps it's a figure of speech for when you really like something but don't openly express it."

"Makes sense," Juan agrees.

"Morris. Is it really fair Legion robbed you and your mother of your dignity? You were the Ruler's chosen Guardians, now you're Evenrise's newest lowlifes."

"Enough, Chantel," Celia says.

"The harsh truth is that Legion never cared about you two. All the good you and Celia have done—saving lives, swearing oaths, maintaining the peace? You can continue doing that now, but now no matter how much good it does, they'll only see you as petty Slums. If you really want the honor you deserve, then join me in getting rid of them to forge a society that allows you to uphold the oaths you've taken." Chantel reveals a small vial containing a blue liquid. "Let this be the beginning of a great partnership."

Morris's eyes go keen and bright. "What's that?"

"Your mother's dying, Morris. Not from illness, but from Legion's arrogance and mistreatment. She can be saved. All I ask for is your loyalty."

All eyes snap to Morris now. He does not hesitate an instant to save his mother's life; he bends knee to Chantel.

"Morris, no," Celia cries.

"I pledge myself to you from this day, to my final day. Every step, every word, every breath I take shall be in your name." He struggles to say it. "Please save her."

"A simple 'yes' would've sufficed." Chantel is overwhelmed by the flattery. "I'd be a cruel son-of-a-bitch to refuse your noble gesture."

Chantel holds out the vials and Morris extends his hand under them. Chantel only has to drop the vials into his hands, and Celia would be cured.

A crunch from within the fisted palm. She drops the shattered vial and blue liquid over Morris's hand.

"Oops," is all Chantel says.

"Vile witch!" shrieks Celia. "Have you no shame?"

"The point is: The Slum District's my domain. You've played savior long enough."

"Morris?" Celia softly calls to her son. He mutters darkly under his breath.

"You heartless bitch. I'll kill you. I swear, I'll fucking kill you!" Morris angrily lunges at Chantel. He's sucker punched by her two minions—one, then the other.

"Go easy on him, boys, he's having a hard day."

"He's never been double-teamed by us before?" Yuan holds Morris while Juan punches him several times over.

"We've been told we're pretty rough," Juan adds as the duo continues the assault. They finish by throwing him through the cottage wall. He lies there, buried beneath the rubble.

"Morris!" Celia cries. Kasen, Daphne, and Gunter quickly go to dig him out.

"Enjoy the time you've left, Celia. Oh… and thank you for your service."

Juan and Yuan laugh as Chantel waggles her fingers, and they leave.

"I'm fine," Morris grumbles. He pulls himself from the debris, disregarding his friends' help as he limps down the street to an unoccupied alley. He beats his hands on the fence that imprisons them and curses at the sky.

The humans follow Kika as she strolls through the fortress's underground corridors. Rounding a corner, they spot a pair of Sigil-bearers patrolling ahead.

"Let's find another way," Heather suggests, but Kika appears disappointed. Not with Heather—but the guards.

"Are they even trying?" She angrily marches over.

"What are you doing?" Heather whispers sharply, but goes ignored.

"What the actual hell, guys?" The armed guards blankly stare as this Devil girl stalks in from nowhere to give them what-for. "You think playing hide-n'-seek is a joke? Well, it's not, so if you're not gonna take it seriously, don't play. When I count to ten, you better be hiding."

Kika closes her eyes and counts. The guards awkwardly look at another before drawing their weapons.

Before the Sigil-bearers attack, sharp claws extend from behind and puncture their backs, repeatedly slamming them into the wall until they're little more than battered corpses.

"Serves you right." Kika sticks her tongue out at the disfigured bodies. The claws retract.

"What was that?" Heather shrieks as she and the other humans approach.

"What was what?" she replies.

"You're a difficult one to track, Devil child." Corrinne appears before them, her claws slick with the blood of the Sigil-bearers she killed.

Heather gasps. "Corrinne?"

"Why does everyone have cool names except me?" Kika pouts. "I want one, too. Maybe something like Heather."

"MY name?"

"Your name's Heather? Huh. Thought it was something else." She sighs. "Guess I'll stick with Kika."

"Ahem. Ladies," Corrinne interrupts them. "Don't you think now's a good time to get you off this icky island?"

"What about Tauro? What was that freaky thing you did with your fingers?"

"Does it really matter right now? Follow me, lovely. Unless you'd rather spend the night?" Corrinne winks at Heather.

Kika, for her part, sees nothing wrong with it. She flashes her sunniest smile. "OK."

"Wait a second," Heather whispers, grabbing her by the arm. "I don't know how you function, but can we really trust this Apparition? She killed her own men. She could be leading us into a trap."

"That sounds fun," Kika decides, and follows after Corrinne.

Heather exchanges looks with her fellow humans as the two Bizarre trot away. "It's not like we have a choice," she sighs, finally, and they all fall into step.

Corrinne keeps her word. She leads them to an underground canal, where a small raft gently bumps into a dock.

"The winds should sail you back to the coast, hopefully," the panther says. "But my offer's still available if you ever decide to come back." She caresses Heather's cheek. Heather cringes away from her.

Kika, on the other hand, pouts. She doesn't want Corrinne to go. "Can't you play a little longer?"

"So sorry, Devil child, but I did have a splendid time." She pats Kika's head. "Your companion's waiting for you."

"My who? Oh, yeah. Guess I should see if he's still terrible at hide-n'-seek."

Kika hops on the raft with the humans. Corrinne unties the rope; they float down the canal and out into the sea. The morning sky welcomes them as they exit the canal tunnel.

"Apparition... I mean, Kika." Heather speaks sincerely now under the open sun. "I never thought I'd be saying this to one of your kind, but I'm grateful to you. We all are. You saved our lives, even if your methods were unorthodox. The other humans are grateful, too."

"Meh. You guys are OK at hide-n'-seek," Kia replies with a wide grin.

Kasen opens his eyes to the sounds of squawking gulls, and waves washing on the land.

How isn't he dead, he wonders. When he tries to move, a sharp pain shoots through his body.

"Unwise to be hasty with that wound." A woman with platinum blond hair, dark blue eyes, and an elegant battle gown stands next to where he lies. Beyond her lingers a dark, muscular man standing at the coastline, gazing toward the horizon.

"Who are you?" Kasen asks.

"It's of no importance," she replies.

"OK? Thanks for saving me."

"I had little involvement with your revival. What saved your life was the Divine Blade you carry." She reveals the black sword, held by her own hand.

"The what?"

"You're a foolish boy to carry something you have no knowledge of. The Divine Blades are weapons crafted during the First Era and given to the Blessed People. Their time was nearing its end, so this was their prayer for maintaining stability. The blades are enhanced by the power of the Divine Lord's blessing and their sole purpose is to destroy anything that poses a threat to existence. But even that wasn't enough to prevent the wars that spawned the terrible scourge we call Evil. It corrupted and destroyed all it touched, but it was finally sealed by a specially forged Divine Blade."

"That's a lot to take in," Kasen says, astounded. For a second, he forgets the pain still weighing him down. "I don't know anything about Divines or blessings, or Aura. But if this Evil's sealed, why's there still... Evil?"

"It was sealed, not destroyed," she answers. "And even Evil has worshippers. They eagerly wait for its seal to break so they may descend upon the lands again. There's only one person capable of destroying it entirely: The Vanquisher."

"The Vanquisher?"

"The only being blessed with the power to do so and bring the Era of Eternal Peace. For years, I've searched for their whereabouts, only to find they died while still in the womb. And now, with the armies of Evil regrouping, it won't be long before they bring about the End of Days."

"I won't let that happen." Kasen rises to his feet.

"What can an ordinary boy do?"

"I don't know, but I'm not going down without a fight, either. I think I'm doing alright for an ordinary boy."

"I see. Maybe your sheer determination allows you to wield this blade. I wish I could remember that feeling." The sword disappears from her hand, and reappears in Kasen's. "Or maybe you're just an ordinary boy."

"There's also my friends. I couldn't imagine making it this far without them."

The man returns to the woman's side. "He appears to be functioning on his own. It's time we moved on."

"I've a small favor to ask." Kiera hands Kasen a small round rusty shield. "If you manage to encounter the one referred to as Sacred Born in your travels, give this to her. Tell her she still has a long way to go."

"S—Sure." Kasen takes the shield.

"I wish you and your friends good fortune in these uncertain times."

The pair departs. Kasen studies the black sword once more. He wonders just how ordinary he is.

NOT SO HARMONIOUS, AFTER ALL

Ashli and Eugene return to Harmony to see Feral putting village residents in chains. A woman pleads for them to stop. She is slain silent. It's a fate she shares with the United Apparition soldiers that lie slaughtered throughout the village.

"Why are we busting our asses for these Sigil punks, anyways?" a Feral complains. "These humans should be ours to use." As he tries groping a woman, he's pushed away by one of his comrades.

"Keep your mingy hands off. Tauro demanded they be unspoiled."

"Fuck Tauro and his overly desperate attempt to rejoin the Sigil. We've been slaving away for those island pricks for years, and all for nothing. I say we make our own army, take these lands for ourselves."

His outcry sparks dissent among the Feral. Some agree; some don't. Their dispute quickly turns violent, and Ashli and Eugene observe the fighting from behind a wall of shrubs.

"So Tauro's showing his true colors," says Eugene. "Even his own men don't trust him."

"Shouldn't you be rescuing your human comrades?" asks Ashli.

"There's quite a few of them. Shouldn't we wait for your friend before acting rashly?"

"Waiting takes too long."

Having said so, Ashli emerges from the bushes. The Feral pause as they see her approach.

"Move aside," she orders, and nothing else.

"She's a dumb little girl overstepping her boundaries. What you gonna do if we don't?" are the Feral's last words after Ashli draws her sword and quickly cuts them down.

The others attack, but are no match. The remaining Feral who charges her blindside is caught by Eugene. He overpowers the Feral, positioning their own knife deep into their neck. Then he tosses the body aside, and gives Ashli a nod of approval she returns. They make quick work of freeing the humans from their chains.

"We have to leave before Tauro returns," a freed prisoner warns.

Eugene shakes his head. "Not until that bastard returns my daughter and the others."

Daphne screams in horror as she and Gunter step from the forest— only to be greeted by the sight of bodies everywhere.

"What have you done?" Gunter shrieks.

"You're just in time." Eugene cracks his knuckles. The next thing they know, Daphne and Gunter are bound in the castaway shackles.

"Thought we'd be in chains before you returned?" Eugene interrogates the frightened Apparitions.

"Why did you kill them?" Daphne weeps. "Those were good, kind, innocent people."

"Blame Tauro's men. This village is built to lure people in with lies of safety and protection so they can sell us away. You've one chance to tell us where Tauro's taken my daughter and the others before I start breaking bones."

"We swear we don't know anything," Gunter cries. "We were waiting for Kasen so we could look for the humans together, but we never saw him, so we went ourselves."

"Your friend led him away from the village to assassinate him," Eugene barks.

"Morris would never. Tauro's a wise man, and is teaching Morris to quell his anger after Celia passed away," Daphne protests.

"And you believed him," Ashli coldly replies.

"Please let us speak with Tauro," Daphne asks her. "This all has to be a misunderstanding."

Eugene's eyes narrow with derision. "Your shackles aren't coming loose a moment before."

The humans go to work. They remove the slain bodies so as not to draw Tauro's suspicions, and he arrives the next morning, finding the village as he had instructed his men to leave it: cleared-out.

Upon entering his home, however, he sees Daphne and Gunter bound to his bed. The humans quickly block Tauro's only means of escape.

"Good morning, Tauro." Eugene says, as he, Ashli, and the remaining villagers trap him inside.

"And you, Eugene," Tauro darkly answers. "Is there a reason for trapping me in my own home?"

"Tauro," breathed Daphne. "Please tell them Harmony isn't selling people away."

"Tell them they're wrong about Morris and you," pleads Gunter. "He wouldn't kill Kasen, and you're a kind and honest man."

Tauro blinks away the shock. "Goodness—is that what you think of me now?"

"See? We told you—" Gunter is interrupted by a sharp something Tauro sticks into his side.

"Gunter!" Daphne cries as he collaspses.

"Not sure why I let you two live this long," Tauro hums. "No point worrying about it now, when everything's already in motion."

"What are you going on about?" Eugene demands.

"You humans don't scare easy, but that doesn't make you any less pathetic. Humans are worth a fortune in the trade. I had my spies inform nearby Feral camps about Harmony, and that's all they needed to hear to come blindly charging in. I needed you humans to believe that nowhere outside the city was safe. Those Legion idiots sent their best men here while the rest go on a suicide mission somewhere in the Uncharted Territories. That fool, Morris, is on his way to Evenrise. His sacrifice will pave the road for me to become the Ruler of the new era."

"Yours is a recycled scheme of the Feral who failed before you," Ashli coldly observes.

"You refer to my brother, Garrick. Not one smart bone in his body—but nonetheless, he served his purpose."

"You used your own brother in pursuit of power?" Eugene says, aghast. "Do Feral have a low?"

Ashli draws her sword. "This Feral annoys me."

"You will sheathe your sword, Sacred Born. That is, if Eugene values his bitch of a daughter's life. I'll be leaving here without being followed."

Eugene growls. "Let him go. Even if he's lying, I won't let this monster use my daughter as leverage. But don't assume you've won, either, Tauro."

Unbelievably, Ashli sheathes her sword, and steps aside.

The humans, too, part, allowing Tuaro to leave unharmed. Daphne and Gunter are unshackled, and she immediately tends to her wounded friend.

Kasen arrives sometime later to find Harmony in ruins. The remaining residents gather what they can find for supplies. Still in a great deal of pain, he uses a tree to support him, before staggering his way into the village.

"Eugene," a worker calls, pointing at Kasen. "It's another Apparition."

He orders a few of his neighbors to stop their foraging to assist, and they half-escort, half-carry the wounded Kasen to their leader.

"You're alive?" Eugene marvels. "Albeit hardly."

"It's a rather complicated story," Kasen fobs. He casts his eyes around the scattered remains of tents and fires. "What happened here?"

"Kasen. Tauro's manipulated Morris into doing something awful," Daphne says, putting down a crate, her voice hoarse. "He wants to take over Evenrise."

"*Tauro.*" Kasen clenches his fists, but his head hangs low. "We had the responsibility of keeping this village safe. We failed."

"There's still time." Daphne tries comforting him. "You can stop Tauro and bring Morris to his senses."

"You may want to rest a bit before you injure yourself more," Eugene suggests.

"He prefers to have his ass kicked sooner rather than later," Ashli says.

"Yeah," Kasen admits, face scrunching with pain, letting the remarks sink in. "He nearly killed me."

"So what—you're just giving up?" Eugene barks. "You searched for my daughter, even after my being cruel to you. You've taken a lifetime oath as a soldier, and no matter how grim the situation may be, you've sworn to uphold it."

"I will. Of course I will." Kasen regains some composure. "I'll set this right somehow. Ashli. We're going to stop Tuaro from hurting anyone else."

"I suppose we are," she replies.

"And Kika. Wait, where's Kika?"

"HELLO, friends!" she shouts, arriving at the head of a gaggle of once-captured humans.

Heather runs to her father, embracing him tightly. For a moment, the ruined Harmony is full of loved ones reuniting.

"Are you alright?" Eugene takes a relieved look at her.

She smiles at Kika. "Thanks to her."

"Guess there are some good Apparitions, after all." Eugene laughs.

"Where have you been?" Ashli asks.

"I don't remember," she answers honestly. "It was a fun game, though. What are we playing next, companion?"

"We're going after Tauro. He's going to do something terrible if he isn't stopped."

"You mean something like cheating?" Kika shrieks. "Let's go teach that son-of-a-bitch a painful lesson. I can smell his cheating ass from here. C'mon."

"They're an odd trio," Eugene mutters, bemused, as they the three hurry in pursuit of Tauro and Morris.

The sun shines over Evenrise. Morris is just inside its line of sight.

"Celia. I swear you will be avenged."

CELIA PT. 1

"**I** trust you're prepared," Gyra infers of a nervous-looking Celia as she stands in her Royal Guard uniform.

"I hope," she replies, but her anxiety's gripped every inch of her face.

"You needn't worry. You were chosen by the Ruler herself. You've proven worthy of your role."

"Mommy, when can we go home?" A toddler tugs his mother's garments.

"Be patient, Morris," she urges.

"Today's important for you, too, youngling." Gyra pats Morris's head.

"You've shaped her into fine warrior," Polina whispers to Andre. They watch on, standing in formation with several other Legion officials.

Andre fondly shakes his head. "It was her own discipline that earned her this title."

"Hush now," Polina tuts. "Our Ruler approaches."

Everyone salutes a gracefully dressed Kiera. Her newborn tucked in her arms, protected by a woven blanket.

"Lady Kiera." Celia, at the head of the ranks, bows.

"Raise your head," she kindly replies. "It should be I who is bowing to you."

"I—You—You shouldn't. It wouldn't be right of you," Celia stutters.

"I've chosen you to be my Royal Guardian to preserve the Era of Peace. I've much faith in you."

Celia quickly bows again, and pledges a lifelong oath to Kiera. Kiera's newborn begins to whimper through the last of the vows.

"She's beautiful," Celia swears, as her eyes meet with the child's.

Kiera considers it, and the infant in her arms. "I've given her the name Ashli in honor of the human who saved my life."

"Have you been watching and listening, Morris?" Celia kneels down to her son. "We're now sworn Royal Guards. We live to serve and protect the Ruler. When her child reaches the proper age, she'll take her mother's place. As you'll do the same with me."

"But where will you go?" Morris asks.

Celia brushes her son's head. "Don't worry. Whatever happens, know I'll always be with—"

Celia starts choking uncontrollably. Each cough covers her fingers in blood. Her hands begin trembling.

"Mommy?" Morris begs as his mother turns pale and collapses.

Morris closes his mind to the eerie memory from long ago.

"Having second thought, Morris?" Tauro had only recently caught up with him.

His voice and thoughts are dark. "Legion's gone unpunished long enough."

"Before you embark, allow me to bestow a gift upon you. Hold out your weapon." Morris does as requested. Tauro holds a black book over it and, after he mutters a short chant, the mace radiates black and crimson Aura."Your potential no longer has limits," Tauro says. "Legion will feel the full wrath of your vengeance. Go now—you are ready."

"Thank you, Tauro. For everything you've done for me," Morris said before departing down the final stretch of land toward Evenrise.

It has been a slower workday than usual for the Legion soldier at the main gates of Evenrise.

Vonnie—still, alas, a novice in Sloth's eyes—had been assigned to help Apparitions migrating to the city weeks ago. "I guess this is better than meditating for hours on end," she sighs.

"Try being a Noble representative." In a rare stroke of luck, the Nobles had also assigned Melony to the job. The pair became acquainted over time.

Vonnie halfheartedly smiles. "Must be nice."

"Well, if you like narcissists and terrible food," Melony jokes.

"Sounds like my kind of people." The two girls share a laugh.

"I've been wanting to ask you about Kasen. What's your relationship?" Melanie hesitantly asks.

"We're just close friends," Vonnie replies.

"Nothing else?"

"Just close friends," she says again.

"Of course." Melony sighs reluctantly.

"Why do you ask?"

"No reason. I've a quick errand to run." Melony excuses herself.

That was weird,' Vonnie thinks, but then redirects her attention to a waiting migrant. A tall, dark Apparition boy.

"Welcome to Evenrise," she greets him, her usual speech. "You've traveled alone, I see. You must not have had much trouble, especially with Feral running rampant. Most are eager to enter the city, but to get you situated, I need to ask a few questions. Have you migrated here to enlist as a United Apparition soldier, or do you have any skill sets that may benefit them?"

"I cook," the migrant boy says.

"OK...Anything else?"

"I cook...well."

"Well, we may have something for you, then. Follow me."

"Things really have changed," the migrant boy murmurs as he takes in the environment of Evenrise.

"It's hard to believe," Vonnie concurs. "Evenrise had such a strict social system. It was cruel to those who barely got by. A good friend of mine worked tirelessly to make them see the error of their ways. People are learning how to grow stronger by working together. I hope he returns from his assignment soon. Maybe I'll introduce you to him."

"Maybe..." The migrant boy seems hesitant. Vonnie doesn't think much of it. Lots of people are nervous upon entering the great gates.

"You're the first cook to migrate here. I'm sure the local cooks would love sharing recipes," Vonnie chatters as she and the migrant boy reach the food court, hoping to put him a little more at ease.

"Vonnie! You're just in time." Polina waves to her. "We're experimenting with some new recipes. Care to test a taste?"

"Of course! But I think he might be a better judge than me." She presents the migrant boy. "He says he was a cook before he came here, and I thought you two might need and extra pair of hands."

"Maybe…" Andre's suspicion, always reliable, creeps in. "You seem familiar. Have we met, young man?"

"Stop being paranoid," Polina sighs. "Excuse my husband; he thinks he knows everyone. Will you hurry up?" she yells at a passing worker, who struggles to carry a heavy cauldron filled with soup.

"That reminds me—I never got your name. I'm Vonnie." She holds out a hand to the migrant boy.

The servant fumbles the pot. Spilling its contents all over the ground.

"Damn you, Ralphie! Unbelievable. A week's worth of experimenting ruined." Polina scolds him, but his attention is locked on the migrant. "Sometimes I don't know why I even bothered with you. You're hopeless. Not a real soldier, not a real cook, not a real rogue, not even a kitchen wor—"

"You're—you're Morris," Ralphie blurts, pointing with a trembling finger. "From the Band of Rouges."

Polina turns sharply to him. "What? *Morris?*"

"So it is you," Andre exhales.

"Why didn't you say so?" snaps Polina.

"You told me to stop being paranoid," Andre growls.

Morris apprehends Vonnie. Holds a knife at her throat.

"Andre. Polina. Take me to Gyra. I don't want to hurt her if I don't have to."

"What on earth do you think you're doing, Morris?" Polina shrieks.

"What neither of you will. You should be leading a rebellion against Legion after all they've done."

"Easy, Morris." Andre tries to calm him. "If you're angry, make sure you take it out on the right people."

"I will once you take me to Gyra."

"What do we do, Andre?" Polina whispers to her husband.

"Give him what he wants. The boy clearly has issues to take care of."

"Shut up and start walking." Still holding Vonnie hostage, Morris follows Andre and Polina while Ralphie is left behind.

Morris hadn't lied to Vonnie about being a cook. He learned this skill—and many others—while still a child. When Celia fell ill, Andre had immediately put him into military training.

"When can I eat?" A young Morris complains in the midst of his lesson.

"If you focused on training as much as your hunger, you'd already be Royal Guard material," Andre replies. "Now, again."

"I'll show you..."

Morris and Andre spar with training weapons. Whenever Morris grows sluggish in stance or reckless in his attacks, Andre reprimands him with a hit to his legs, arms, or head.

"You're leaving yourself wide open. Stay vigilant."

"How's he doing?" A weakened Celia uses a training totem for support.

"What are you doing out of bed?" Polina hurries to assist her. "You should be inside resting."

"Please. I need to see him," Celia coughs. "He needs to see that I'm here for him."

Polina nods. "He'll grow to become a fine Royal Guard. I'm certain of it."

It's enough to make Celia smile, at least. They continue watching Morris train under Andre until a squad of Legion officials interrupts.

"This is a private session. Why have you disturbed us?" Andre questions them.2

"Royal Guard Celia." An official hands her a rolled letter. "By order of the Fairest Council, you and your kin are hereby relieved of your duties, and are to relocate off Academy grounds. Effective immediately."

"What?" Andre and Polina see Gyra's left his signature stamp at the bottom of the letter.

"A unanimous vote declared Celia unfit for the responsibilities given to her."

"A vote? I'm a member of the Council! Why wasn't I informed?" barks Andre.

"You'll have to take the matter to them. Either way, it's their decision, it's final, and we're authorized to use force if necessary." The officials prepare to draw their weapons if given cause.

"This is outrageous. If it's a fight you want—" Polina shrieks. She's calmed by Celia.

"We'll leave immediately." She bows. "Thank you."

"Mom, don't let them do this," Morris protests. "Ever since you got sick, they've—"

"I know. But your safety is all that matters. We can solve this matter without the need for violence."

"I'm going to speak with the Council immediately," Andre swears, cursing up a storm as he departs for the Academy.

"Our home is off Academy grounds," Polina assures them. "Please stay with us until we figure out what's going on."

The Fairest Council holds their meeting in the Academy archives. Their newest member, Edwin, loses himself in history novels. Gyra and France sit at the council table in the center of the room.

"Is something troubling you, Fairest Gyra?" France asks, noticing his mellow expression.

"How long have we been allies, Commander France?" he asks.

"Nearly three decades, I estimate."

"And all this time, you've never questioned my decisions, even if they went against your beliefs. Do you follow me for loyalty, or fear?"

"Forgive me, Your Fairest, but I don't understand." France repositions herself.

"What the young Apparition Kasen said when he was on trial. 'Doing the right thing.' I believed I acted with the best intentions when we enforced the social laws. Were you as surprised as I was when he exposed how much misery it had caused to the people? You voted that he live. Why?"

"He was telling the truth, Your Fairest," France replies. "None would take a risk such as his just for a good laugh. You've always sought after the greater good. Your decisions may not always be just, but we learn from our mistakes and strive to work harder."

"Apologies, Commander France. I'm afraid it's too late for me to learn from mine."

The archive doors creep open—and through them come Vonnie, Andre, and Polina.

"Were we expecting guests?" Edwin lowers his book, uneasy.

"Andre, Polina. Is there something wrong?" France asks

"It's all right." Gyra rises from his chair. "I know you've come, young Morris."

"You." Morris is as cold as a winter storm. He reveals himself from behind his hostages, remembering Gyra as the man who condemned him and his mother to an awful fate.

"I should've known that the minute Kiera left with her daughter, those vultures would start changing things for the worse." Andre grumbles as he builds a small fire.

Polina consoles him. "Then we'll just have to send those vultures flying."

After the reformed government of Evenrise enforced its social laws, things changed for Morris and his family. They discharged Andre and Polina, and abruptly relieved many other Commoners of their duties just as the cold season brewed overhead. Celia's condition had only worsened.

"We've tried. Many have tried. And look what's happened. We're slain in the streets or deported to the Slum District. If you didn't believe in hell before, it's on the other side of the fences. Soldiers are free to raid our homes. Now we've little to live off of, and Celia." He peeks into the other room where Morris tends to his mother. "She won't last like this," he says quietly.

"We've lived through worse. Will you have a little faith," Polina castigates him, before she enters Celia and Morris's room.

FOREVER WILL END

"These rags are cold. Warm them for her, young man." She hands Morris a new set of rags and he leaves to go warm them at the fire.

"How do I look?" Celia can barely speak the words.

"Save your strength." Polina brushes over Celia's forehead. "You'll overcome this and resume your role as Royal Guard."

Celia takes her hand. "Polina. He's the only reason I continue holding on. We both know I don't have much time left but when it happens—when that time comes—please relay a message to him." She whispers into Polina's ear just as someone knocks on the door. Andre opens it to Gyra, accompanied by his guards.

"To what do we owe this visit?" Andre grumbles, not thrilled to see him.

"We've received word you're providing shelter for illegal residents of the Commoners District. We're here to escort them to where they properly belong."

"Gyra, haven't you done enough to them?" Andre asks, but it's sharper than it is pleading. "What more can you take?"

"If you resist our efforts to uphold order, I'll have no choice but to convict you and your wife of harboring illegal residents. You know the penalty for living outside of your District. I don't want that to happen to Celia and her son. Don't make this any harder, Andre."

An angry Morris charges at Gyra. He's caught by Polina before he can make matters worse, and he sobs, going limp in her arms.

"You must be so proud," Polina says, staring at the Councilor, her voice like ice.

"Everyone, please." Celia pulls herself from bed. "Andre. Polina. We're thankful for hospitality you've provided."

"Mom, we can't. If we go, you'll..."

"Come, Morris. Before we overstay our welcome."

"My guards will escort you to your proper district," Gyra ensures. "Celia. We haven't forgotten your service to Evenrise and its people. A small cottage was made for you and your son."

It was from this point forward, Morris knew, that he would hate Legion with all his head and all his heart.

CELIA PT. 2

"**S**melled your cheatin' ass from ten miles away, you cheatin' ass," Kika shouts when she, Kasen, and Ashli manage to catch up to Tauro.

Tauro laughs hysterically. "You three are more of a pain in the ass than I was informed. Morris didn't have what it takes to kill his friend. The Devil girl's escaped my grasp, and I just don't plain like you, Sacred Born. Despite your annoyances, you're too late. Morris has already entered the city. With the enchantment I bestowed on his mace. The Aura created from his anger will be absorbed, and once it has enough, Evenrise will be nothing but rubble and ash. When word spreads of how I single-handedly destroyed Evenrise, my ascension to rule over these lands will be assured."

"Why reveal your master plan? All we have to do is inform Morris," says Kasen.

"You've seen how broken the boy is. He's too angry to care. But I'll spare him the time of dealing with you brats." Tauro draws his battle-axe.

"We'll convince him after we're done with you, Tauro." Kasen prepares to face him.

"How much more time do you intend to waste here?" Ashli steps in front. "Go save your friend and that city you care so much about."

Kasen nods after a moment. There isn't time to argue. He wants to tell her to be careful, but can't muster the courage.

Tauro allows Kasen to run past him, puffed up with the belief that he'd be too late to do anything.

"We fight, Kika." Ashli draws her sword.

"I call everything below the waist. That's how you fight, right?"

"Sacred Born? Your title will disappear when my Era as Ruler begins."

FOREVER WILL END

Kasen makes haste through Evenrise. It was many years ago that Celia given him a very important task.

No one had seen young Morris for days—not since Chantel and her henchman had beaten him in his own home.

Kasen, Daphne, and Gunter resume their daily activities, waiting for his return. Celia suffers immensely in his absence. Her days spent groaning in pain, her nights weeping for her son. But one morning—not so terribly unlike the others—Kasen's role in life would drastically change.

"Be careful with her," Daphne warns, as Gunter enters the cottage carrying a sick little girl. He gently lays her on the floor. She wears a similar necklace to the one Kasen wore when he arrived at the Slum District. Only hers bore the name *Vonnie.*

"Let her lie in bed," Celia says. With Daphne and Gunter's help, Celia and Vonnie switch places. Vonnie's panting is paced, deep, and agonized.

"Is there anything we can do?" Daphne asks.

Celia shakes her head. "I'm sorry. In her condition, she won't last the night. All we can do is provide her comfort in her final hours."

"Who's that?" Morris unexpectedly appears at the door. But he's changed. Celia saw black Aura coming from her son. She was frightened of him. "Why's she lying in my mother's bed?" he demands.

"Morris," Celia whimpers.

"We found her in the alleys; we couldn't leave her to die," says Gunter.

"She's going to die. You're wasting time." The room gasps at Morris's harsh words.

"How dare you speak that way?" his mother scolds him.

"When will you people understand? These so-called law-abiding citizens want us dead. The Slum District is a way for us to kill each other so they don't have to live with the guilt of killing us themselves. Everything you fought for, Mother, didn't matter. I refuse to live this way another second. We're busting out of this hell hole."

"How?" Daphne asks.

"There's an Apparition group that lives well beyond the city. I met them. They're fighting for the freedoms we deserve. This is our chance to finally make something of ourselves."

"What about the people too weak to follow you? The same people you're taking care of now?" Celia argues. "Morris. This path you've chosen. I can't go with you."

Morris kneels down to his mother. He takes her hands; the warmth her son's touch had always given her is no longer there.

"I promise to come back for you. I'll free the Slum District, and turn Evenrise into something better."

Celia pulls her hands away. She stares deeply into Morris's cold eyes. "What have they done to you?"

"We leave now." With nothing more to say, Morris exits the cottage.

"What do we do?" Gunter asks. "Many residents depend on us. If we leave, who knows what will happen?"

"But Morris has a point," replies Daphne. "There's a rumor that they're fortifying the fences into stone walls. And who knows when Legion soldiers will come for us?"

"They'll die without our help," Gunter argues.

"They are *with* our help, and I don't want to end up dying next," Daphne snaps back.

"...I don't, either," Gunter murmurs—and no more.

"Go." Celia speaks softly. "Don't allow your fears to sway you. You both possess remarkable talent to help others. You should share that talent with the world. I've delayed my fate for far too long. Just promise to look after my son. Something sinister has taken hold of him."

Daphne and Gunter bow their heads. "Thank you for everything. We'll never forget what you've taught us." Gunter says, before they leave the cottage to catch up to Morris. Kasen, however, remains.

"Come closer." Celia gestures to Kasen. He sees Vonnie still clinging to life.

"I feel in your heart you wish to save her. Morris used to not sleep for days, not until he knew every Slum resident was cared for. The only person he couldn't help was me." Celia chuckles, but it's a dark and ironic mirth. "I can't stop you from following your heart. Sometimes we must be willing to sacrifice a part of ourselves to do the right thing. Why I allow you this choice and not Morris is because he's let himself be led astray from what he's been taught. There's only one way to save her. I can't say I approve of it, but I'll pray for your safe return. I'll keep watch over her."

Kasen nods, and departs for the south end of the Slum District.

"I'm bored, what sounds fun?" Juan wonders as he and Yuan stand outside Chantel's tent.

"We could collect debt payments," Yuan suggests.

"That's work. Which is also fun, but not enough."

"Make people fight to the death for our amusement?" Yuan suggests again.

"Hm. Getting warmer."

"We can smear each other with frosting again."

"Fine. As long as you don't use your tongue, it's disgusting." They enter Chantel's home.

Kasen listens in on their conversation from outside the tent, filled with doubts and second-thoughts about what he is about to do.

"Seriously? I said no tongue!" Juan snaps as he and Yuan become entwined in a schoolyard brawl.

"Play nice, boys," Chantel says from the comfort of her chair. Her other servants hand-feed her fruit and serve her wine, as they often do.

"Excuse me. Chantel?" Kasen enters unannounced. Juan and Yuan quickly react by pinning him to the ground.

"You dare enter Lady Chantel's home without approval, you shit?" Juan snaps.

"A painful death is the proper punishment for disrespecting our Lady," says Yuan.

"Settle down, boys," Chantel interrupts. Kasen's released from Juan and Yuan's grip, but they keep a sharp eye on him. "Obviously he's got something uninteresting to say, so go on and speak."

"There's this girl," Kasen says nervously. "She's really sick. Please. You're the only one who can save her—and many others—with your medicine."

Chantel yawns at his plea. "See? I told you it'd be uninteresting. Get rid of him."

Juan and Yuan grab hold of Kasen; he struggles to break free of them.

"We're killing him, right?" Yuan asks.

"Duh," Juan scoffs.

"I know you can be kind," Kasen yells. "Just like when I first arrived here!"

"Hold on," Chantel says, and Juan and Yuan cease their efforts to drag Kasen away.

"I was attacked. I should be dead. Someone—I'm not sure who—saved me. I just thought if anyone could've..."

"Lady Chantel. What's this brat babbling about?" Juan asks.

"I say we cut out his tongue first," Yuan says.

"Leave us." Without question, the boys release Kasen, bow, and exit her home. Her servants scurry out, as well.

"What ARE you babbling about?" Standing from her chair, Chantel circles around Kasen.

"I'm not sure how to explain it," Kasen replies. "Whoever saved me, I'd be in their debt. I didn't come here to start anything. I just want to help these people. I just want to be able to do the right thing."

Chantel reveals two blue vials of medicine. "Those sick people have a rare illness that causes them to produce more Aura than they can withstand. This is a special Aura blend that stabilizes it. One bottle is worth more than double the lives of everyone here. How do you intend to purchase them?"

"I—I don't know. I don't have anything," Kasen babbles.

"So, let me get this straight. You barge into my home, chest out, muscles flexed, cock erect, and you hoped that I'd be so kind to hand you a life-saving solution?"

"I—I just want..."

"Yeah, yeah. You're a champion of the people. Lucky for you, I've never found value in trinkets, odds and ends. That sort of thing. There's something far valuable, and you just happen to be full of it... life. I need lives like yours at my disposal. Those who live by a moral code are always valuable to some extent, but are you really willing to sell your life just to save a few half-dead Slum residents? Because there was this little bitch and his mom who..."

Kasen interrupts. "I was there."

"Oh. Well, so much for an interesting story." With no tricks, Chantel gives Kasen the medicine.

He almost can't believe it. Kasen quickly returns to the cottage. He's in such a daze, he almost fumbles the vials when he takes them out of his pocket.

"Careful, now. She only needs a little." Celia places a few small drops into Vonnie's mouth. She brushes down the girl's sweaty hair. "The rest is up to her now."

"There's enough to save you, too. You'll be well again, and Morris can—" Celia returns the vial to Kasen.

"You're a brave young man, but my place is with my son, even now when he's lost. You must become the hope for these people. I know one day you'll be reunited. Please bring him back to the light?"

Kasen nods as he wipes the tears from his eyes.

"Please allow me to be alone for a while." Kasen helps Celia back into bed and carries the unconscious Vonnie piggyback. She smiles at Kasen as he wipes away more tears. A hand gently travels over his cheek.

"It's OK. I'm going to be with my son now. I'll be waiting for you to return him to me."

Kasen nods once more and leaves with Vonnie. He closes the cottage door. They'd never, he feared, open it again.

Slum residents gather around the cottage. They look at Kasen with uncertainty. Vonnie's panting has dramatically calmed since ingesting Chantel's medicine, and her deathly paleness recedes.

Staring back at them all with newfound confidence, he gives himself over wholly to his new role. Someway, somehow, he would heal the Slum, and honor Celia's will.

At the great wall surrounding Evenrise, Morris, Daphne, Gunter, and a few other Slum residents are in process of making their escape. Apparitions on the other side of the fence pry the barbed wire over the top, and toss over a rope for them to climb.

"Where's Kasen?" Morris asks, realizing he hadn't followed with Daphne and Gunter.

Gunter startles. "Wasn't he behind us?"

"I think he's staying," Daphne replies.

"What? Why?" shrieks Morris.

"Let's go, people," shouts one of Apparitions waiting for them to climb over.

With no time to wait and wonder, Morris and the others climb over to freedom beyond the city.

CELIA PT. 3

"**G**yra." Morris stares coldly into the eyes of his nemesis. "You took everything. I've come to take it back."

"If your anger's with me, Morris, then don't waste it on the others," Gyra calmly replies.

"So, this is Morris," France muses. "Fairest Gyra has spoken of you."

"Has he told you how 'Fair' he truly is?" Morris dares.

"This behavior is absurdly childish," Edwin intervenes. "There's a healthier and more mature solution to solve this."

"What do you know?" Morris becomes enraged. "You Nobles are just as much to blame as Gyra. Sleeping in your comfortable beds, enjoying your freshly prepared meals. I'm sure it was nice to not have a damn care in the world."

"Something's wrong with him. Observe closely," Andre murmurs, watching the black Aura surround Morris.

Vonnie sees it, too. "What is that?"

"Something that's influencing his anger, I imagine."

"We have to do something before he hurts someone," says Polina.

"I don't know how we'd quell Morris without doing significant harm, and by Gyra's look," Andre warns, "neither does he."

"Excuse me. Excuse me!" Ralphie scrambles through the plaza from person to person, hoping to get anyone's attention. The citizens can't be bothered.

"Why aren't you people listening," Ralphie grumbles—and then spots a familiar face moving with great purpose through the crowd. "Hey! It's you, Kay—? Er. Ko—? Er. Kaw—? What are you doing?"

Kasen approaches Ralphie. "Kasen. And I'm in a hurry."

"You're here for Morris?" he asks.

"He was here?"

"He took Andre, Polina, and that other girl to that Academy. He wanted to settle something with the old people."

"Thanks!" Kasen calls, hurrying past him.

"Tell Polina I'm sorry for spilling the soup," Ralphie yells. But Kasen is already gone.

"Think about what you're doing!" Edwin's the first to try and calm Morris. "Assassinating a Council member on military grounds? You can't expect to make it out of here alive. Whatever happened while you resided in the Slum District is something I pray no one else has to experience. It's easier to hate than forgive, but if you can find solace, you'll be better from it. Be the example Evenrise needs."

It appears as though Edwin's words may have gotten through to Morris—until he throws a knife that sticks deep into Edwin's thigh.

"What the bloody hell?" Edwin shouts, as he falls over, clenching where he was struck. France and Polina immediately tend to him.

"Oh, dear Divine, it hurts so bad. I don't want to die." Edwin whines at the leak of his own blood.

"You're a Nobleman. I suggest you quit bitching like a little bitch," Polina says, as she applies pressure to his leg.

"You're next, Gyra." Morris unsheathes his newly enhanced mace. Gyra stands unarmed before the intruder. "If destroying me will put you at ease, then do what you came here for."

"No! No more violence." Vonnie interjects herself between them. "We're fighting to end violence, don't you remember? If he wants to be our enemy, then we'll treat him like one."

Morris's face is like stone. He turns the mace toward her. "Then be first to fall to my vengeance."

FOREVER WILL END

Kasen bolts through the Academy corridors. He apologizes as he accidently bumps into other Apparitions, running hard for a place he'll never forget: the archive doors.

Two soldiers in gilded armor stop him at the entrance. They cross their spears, preventing Kasen entry. "Entering the archives is forbidden during Fairest Council meetings."

"They're in danger, please let me pass," Kasen pleads.

"No one enters."

"What about the others we allowed just a while ago?" asks the other guard.

"Fairest Gyra made Andre and Polina honorary Council members. This kid is not. Now he can either leave peacefully or in shackles."

"On behalf of Lord Edwin, he may enter the archives." Melony arrives just as Kasen needs a miracle. "I saw that Morris fellow had taken Vonnie hostage. I should've had him apprehend, but we can't afford another widespread panic."

"I have to stop him before he hurts people," blurts Kasen.

"OK. I try to keep this area clear until you do. And Kasen." Melody meets his eye. "Be careful."

"I'll try to be. Thank you."

The guards lift their spears, and now nothing stands in his way.

"Morris!" Kasen's shout draws everyone's attention as he bursts through the archive doors.

"Him again?" Edwin says, surprised.

"You're supposed to be dead," Morris growls. "Suppose you've come all this way because you want me to finish the job."

"I'm here to stop you from doing something you'll regret." Kasen's black sword appears in his hand. "Morris. Tauro's using you so he can rule. He doesn't plan on you living after he gets what he wants."

"So what? At least he didn't abandon me like my so-called friends."

"Now I see. This wasn't about vengeance. Just because Celia passed doesn't mean she abandoned you. You've fooled yourself into blaming everyone else. Morris. You didn't just abandon her. You also abandoned Daphne, Gunter, and everyone you cared for in the Slum District at the time."

"Look at you, Kasen. All high-and-mighty now that you're a Legion soldier. If you had escaped like I did that day, perhaps you'd have a better understanding. Guess you'd rather die alongside the rest of Legion!" Morris yells as he attacks.

Kasen's sword catches it. He knows he must end the battle quickly before Morris's mace is charged with Aura. But Morris is the better fighter, and he knocks Kasen off-balance with a kick that takes him to the ground.

Before the next attack, Kasen kicks at Morris's shin. It delays the blow just enough for him to jump to his feet and initiate a counterattack—but his momentum's cut short when he dives under Morris's fierce mace swing. The two continue clashing, ducking, and parrying one another until it's clear they've become locked in stalemate.

As if sharing the same thought, their heads crash into each other, putting both fighters into a daze. Morris quickly snaps himself out, and lands several painful blows to Kasen, the final of which sends him rolling along into the wall.

"Why are we standing around? We should be helping him!" Vonnie cries.

"Watch and learn," Andre tells her. "This isn't your everyday battle. Your friend is fighting because he knows something we don't. We engage if we absolutely must."

"Why won't you just give up already?" Morris pants, as Kasen gets to his feet. "Do you really want to die that badly?"

"I can't," he says through his pain. "I made a promise to bring you back. You may not be able to tell friend from foe, but that doesn't mean I'm giving up. You're going to have to kill me, Morris. Is that what you really want?"

"Apparently you do. I didn't want it to be this way, but I won't let you stand in the way of my avenging Celia." Morris charges. As he does, Kasen sees the black Aura. He hears it screaming, moaning, for Morris to kill, and let his anger grow.

'Is that what's controlling Morris?' he wonders, a terrible awe. 'Whatever that is wants me gone so it can fully consume him. I won't let that happen.'

Green Aura rises from the black sword, and grants Kasen newfound strength as the weapons collide. The black Aura surrounding Morris shrieks painfully as the green Aura from the black sword consumes it.

"What's happening?" Morris feels himself slipping back to normalcy as the black Aura around him fades.

"Celia chose to go because she wanted to be with you, even after you became a selfish prick." Kasen knocks Morris's mace from his hands. "Get over your vengeance crap already!"

The green Aura transfers to Kasen's fist, which he uses to land a series of straight punches to Morris that send him into a stack of books that topples over him. The instant he disappears beneath their pages, the power the black sword granted to Kasen fades.

"Ugh. What the hell just happened?" Morris digs himself out from the book pile, rubbing his aching head. "Kasen? Andre? Polina? Gyra?"

"Tauro rigged your mace to absorb your anger. Once it was filled, it would've unleashed an explosion meant to destroy Evenrise," Kasen says. "Your quest for vengeance would've taken many innocent people, including the former residents of the Slum District."

"Why would he do that?" Morris gawps.

"I don't know. Because Feral are cruel." As Kasen helps Morris to his feet, black Aura erupts from the mace. The shockwave sends everyone toppling over. Outside, within the city, the citizens look on as the black Aura soars into the sky and blocks out sunlight.

"It must've charged completely," Andre shouts.

"What do we do, how do we stop it?" Kasen shouts back.

"Pray?"

Everything around them shakes violently as a bright light from the mace blinds them. For a terrible instant, they believe it to be the explosion. After a few moments, however, everything calms. Kasen opens his eyes, feeling around to make sure all of him is still there.

"We're alive?"

"Somehow," Vonnie replies.

"H—How?" Morris is on his knees, in awe of Celia's spirit floating above them.

"Celia?" Gyra whispers in shock.

"In all my life," Polina murmurs, awe-struck, "I've never…"

"Are you sure we're not dead?" Vonnie asks.

"Mother… but how?" Morris says, as Celia descends down to him. She looks over to Kasen and smiles. Whatever this is—if it's the real Celia or just some strange Aura-dream—he can't help but smile back.

"I'm sorry," Morris weeps. "I tried so hard to follow in your footsteps; I just wasn't strong enough to do it without you."

Celia's spirit takes Morris's hands, plants a soft kiss on them, and momentarily rests her head on them. Though Morris can't physically feel her touch, he feels the warmth she gives him.

Pulling herself away, Celia picks up the black sword and offers it to Kasen.

"What does she want?" he wonders, staring in wonder.

"She's ready to pass on," Gyra assures him.

"Pass on? She can't," Morris protests, "she just got here!"

"She knows she doesn't belong in this world. Her final wish to reunite with you has been fulfilled. She's at peace now."

"She's waited this whole time for you to come to your senses," Polina adds, eyes flooded with tears. "One couldn't ask for a more loving parent."

"OK… I'm not sure what to do." But all the same, Kasen takes the black sword from Celia. It emits its green Aura and Celia's spirit begins to fade.

"Thank you for staying at my side. I'll never let anger control me again. I promise," Morris says. With one last loving smile, Celia's spirit vanishes.

"She's truly gone," Morris trembles.

"She'll always be with you," Gyra offers. Morris nods to him.

"One thing I don't understand. Morris's mace had absorbed enough of what it needed," France asks, "so why didn't the explosion occur?"

"I've dealt with that particular type of Aura in the past," Gyra answers. "It's an artificial type that only functions so long as it has a host. When Morris's anger quieted, it spiraled out of control and malfunctioned as a result. Once that happened, Morris was able to see more clearly and thus, Celia was able reunite with Morris. Kasen just fulfilled a lost ancient tradition."

"I knew you'd come in handy eventually." Andre pats Kasen on the back.

"What do you mean *eventually*?" Vonnie demands.

"I really screwed up, didn't I?" Morris speaks up from his place on the floor. "I almost killed you all, and allowed myself to be manipulated. I can't begin to tell you how sorry I am."

"I always wondered what would've happened if I left the Slum District with you guys," replies Kasen. "I didn't like Legion any more than you at the time. But I chose to stay because you, Celia, Daphne, and Gunter taught me how to care for others. I'm going to continue to honor Celia's wish. Now that you're under your own influence, you can, too."

Morris smiles. "Yeah. I think I will."

"Aren't we all celebrating a bit too early?" Tauro makes his presence known, standing at the archive door. The guards lie slain on the stairway.

"How'd you get past Ashli and Kika?" Kasen shrieks.

Hours ago, just outside the city of Evenrise, Ashli stood—arms-crossed, sighing—while Kika was slouched on her knees in turmoil.

"You were supposed to hold him," said Ashli.

"I can't. I'm too hungry," Kika whined.

"You know you don't need to eat."

"That's easy for you to say. You don't need to eat," Kika snapped at her, to which Ashli sighed again.

"Do you think they're dead?" Kika asked, receiving a mere grunt from Ashli.

"Wanna see?"

"Gave em the slip," Tauro offers bluntly.

"Still up to no good, Tauro?" says France.

"Can't chat right now, Francey. Too busy conquering this land. Morris, you can go ahead and kill everyone now."

"You don't control me anymore, Tauro," he sharply rebukes.

"Are you sure about that? *Wah! My mommy's dead. Wah! I can't live without her.* You're such a fucking crybaby. Moms die all the time. You Dwellers are so easy to exploit."

"Bastard. I'll show you." Morris grabs his mace. He tries to conjure the power he had before, but is unable to.

"Anger isn't your strength anymore," Kasen reminds him.

"But how can I fight?"

"Well, try thinking of someone or something important to you. Seems to work for me."

"Something important? OK. I'll try," Morris says, as he and Kasen prepare to fight.

"Guess I'll have to find some more obedient Slums," Tauro chuckles, and he draws his battle-axe.

Kasen and Morris attack Tauro head-on. Both jump away as Tauro cleaves his axe into the floor. They try attacking Tauro from both his sides; Morris dodges Tauro's swing, but with his free hand, Harmony's old chief clutches Kasen by his neck and slams him to the ground.

Before Tauro can chop Kasen in two, Morris shoulder-tackles him flat.

"Annoying Slum shit." Tauro quickly recovers, and with his free hand, he hoists Morris high. "Look at you. Weaker and more pathetic than the day I saw you crying for mommy dearest. Drove me nuts to keep hearing you preach about your dreams to shape Evenrise into a better civilization. I've got news for you. It's just a dream!" He throws Morris into Kasen as he attempts to stand, and the two careen into a pile of books and scrolls.

"They need our help," Vonnie says.

"Not yet. Morris needs to learn to fight without his anger," says Gyra.

"Listen to the old man, little girly," Tauro boasts. "These two barely qualify as practice, and I can't be distracted with second-best." He laughs.

"I liked him better when he wasn't so loud," Kasen growls, as he and Morris pull themselves from out under the books.

"He's a lot stronger than he looks," Morris says grimly.

"Is there a way to get in on this guy?"

Morris winces. "Maybe?"

"Slum boys of Evenrise," Tauro sighs. "I'm a merciful Ruler. Serve me willingly and be spared my wrath."

"I'd rather not," replies Kasen.

"You're no Ruler, Tauro," Morris adds.

"You're right," he agrees, and a nasty smile curls across his mouth. I'm your executioner."

FOREVER WILL END

Kasen attacks. But he's left defending as Tauro brings his axe down onto him; he can barely withstand the force of it, and drops heavily to his knees. Tauro takes advantage, and repeatedly kicks Kasen's ribs.

"Any last words before I split you in two?" Tauro darkly ponders.

Kasen grits his teeth. "Finish it."

"With gusto." Tauro brings his axe up.

And here, Kasen smirks. "I wasn't talking to you."

Tauro shrieks as Morris sweeps in and strikes his stomach with the mace.

"Damn Slum rats! Curse you bottom-feeders." Tauro drops to his knees, clenching his leaking wound.

"Remember your dream of being a Ruler? Well, I've got news for you. It's just a dream." Morris strikes Tauro across the face, and he soars into the wall.

"They did it," Polina says, seeing Tauro remain unresponsive.

"You really can take an ass-kicking," Morris chuckles, and assists Kasen back to his feet.

"We knew you could fight without relying on anger." Polina pats Morris's head, and Andre gives him a nod of approval.

"Celia would be proud," Gyra comments.

"Why do you keep showing up at the last second?" Vonnie scolds Kasen.

"I tried getting here faster, honestly."

"Honestly, we should've been dead because of how long you take! Next time we'll start the fight without you."

"C'mon. I'll get here faster next time."

"Fine. But no more dramatic entrances," Vonnie warns him, and shakes her head.

"I'm just glad this ended before things really got out of hand," says Andre.

But it hasn't quite ended—not just yet. There's a wet, sad thumping in the corner of the room.

"Curse you. Curse you. Curse you all!" Tauro yells, sopping blood as he struggles to stand. "Too long have my faith and dedication gone unrewarded. I'm destined to rule these lands. Answer my prayers and give me the power to crush these faithless vermin." Black Aura radiates from him. "You thought he was the only one influenced by anger. There are armies of stronger and more obedient Apparitions. Shame you won't live to see them."

Tauro's moment of triumph ends as quickly as it began—when a sword impales his back and juts out through his stomach.

"You've annoyed me for the last time," says Ashli, as she rips her sword from Tauro's body.

"Hey, companion," Kika hellos happily. "Did ya miss me?"

"Sure, I guess," Kasen replies with a shocked look.

"Ha. You're weird."

Tauro chuckles dismally as a black void forms underneath him and swallows him in. "This is far from over, Legion. I'll return with an army and annihilate this entire city. I swear your deaths will be the most painful."

When he's completely swallowed, the void fades away, and spits him out into a cave far from Evenrise.

"Kill them, slowly, painfully. Make them beg, make them suffer. That is what I'll do when the Will of Evil is under my command. So long as I hold the Gospel of Chaos, my faith will never waiver..."

"T—Tauro?" squeaks a surprised Trexler. "What are you doing here?"

"You." Tauro limps over to Trexler, and pins him against a boulder. "I thought I'd run into your scrawny ass again. I managed to crawl my way out of the fucking gutters after I was exiled by those sex-crazed savages. Then I met you and now I have nothing, again. Are you seeing the problem here?"

"Now's not a good time to be angry," Trexler gasps back at him. "I know there have been a few missteps, but it's only a minor setback."

"All of my men, my brother, the humans! Everything's gone. Now it's your turn."

"I don't remember you being so angry, Tauro." Chantel stands over a rock ledge. Seeing her, he tosses Trexler aside.

"You? You're supposed to be dead," Tauro shrieks.

"I don't know, maybe. A lot of things happen over a decade. Plus with all the other stuff—"

Tauro's gloating laughter interrupts her. "Why should I fear you?" Because of your absence, the cult is locked in an inner power struggle, and that gave me the perfect opportunity to steal Gospel." He reveals the black and red book. "The power of Evil is mine to do with as I will."

"You mean the book you're holding? In your hands? Definitely fake?"

"That's right, and I'll use it to... fake?"

"Poor dumbass Tauro. Unfortunate that you came from a lowborn cultist family. You never got the break you wanted. You're not the first to try and steal the Gospel. Admittedly, it never gets old to see Feral try. But it did eventually get annoying, so fake copies were made and infused with an off-brand Aura. Problem solved."

"You lie," Tauro snarls.

"Did you even read the scriptures? It's complete gibberish."

"Er. I meant to get around to it." Tauro flips to a random page. Its passage reads: *This book is fake and you're and idiot for thinking otherwise.*

"Well, Tauro. You may be lowborn, but you've been the most amusing lowborn." Chantel snaps her fingers. The black book disintegrates, taking Tauro's arm with it. As he yells in pain, he's grabbed and dragged by Juan and Yuan.

"Get your putrid hands off me, you fucking fruits." Tauro can't fight off Juan and Yuan.

"How dare you call us something so foul?" Juan shrieks.

"Fruits suck. Vegetables all the way," says Yuan.

"Agree one hundred percent," replies Juan.

The cave echoes with Tuaro's screams as he's dragged away.

"So, Tauro's dead, like you wanted. What next, Lady Chantel?" Trexler asks.

Chantel reveals a worn book wrapped in chains: the *real* Gospel of Chaos. "Benji and Corrinne's Sigil armies will march upon Evenrise, burn it down, issue forth the End of Days, and thus herald Evil's imminent return. Gonna have to find someone a bit more reliable than Tauro to command their armies, but before that happens, there is somewhere I'd like to visit before the end."

LAST MOMENTS OF JOY

After he has expressed his apologies once more, paid his respects to Celia's final resting place, and said his goodbyes, Morris returns to the ruined Village of Harmony with a promise to keep the humans safe. Thanks to the efforts of Kasen, Ashli, and Kika, fledgling hopes emerge for possible coexistence between humans and Apparitions.

The United Apparition fleet returns a few days after the incident at Harmony Village. Many arrive in bandages, some having lost entire limbs. Sloth is among those unfortunate enough to lose part of his hand. Jaq is rolled in by cart, bandages wrapped around her severe injuries. Omar and Vincent refuse to speak to the public about what had happened.

"Where's Lars?" Kasen is able to squeeze through the crowds to reach Omar. The Commander merely grumbles something, before handing Kasen a folded paper.

His heart sinks when it reads that Lars had been killed in combat. His final request was to have Kasen train under Jaq for a leadership position.

The gourmands of Evenrise prepare a feast for the returning soldiers. Despite all they had experienced, the soldiers ate, drank, and sang without quarter. Most likely because they might not be able to celebrate for a long while. Or ever again.

Kasen isn't as cheerful as the others. He wonders what would've happened to Celia if Morris never came to his senses—or, worse, if he'd won.

"Careful, Kika, you'll choke!" Vonnie scolds. Kika muffles something through her overloaded mouth.

"Hey, you." Melony taps Kasen's shoulder.

"Hi," he says, offering her the seat next to him.

"I would, but I have to get back to Lord Edwin's manor. He still upset about his injury. I just came by to thank you for everything you've done."

"We all did our part."

"You're very noble to not take all the credit, but still, most of us are alive today because of you. I guess I don't have any better way of expressing my gratitude than this."

Melony kisses Kasen hard on his lips.

Kika spits out her food in shock. "Since when are you into girls?"

"I'm just as surprised as she is," Andre seconds.

Polina gives her husband a hard stare.

"What? He didn't have any guy friends."

Kasen's heart races from the start of the kiss, to its end.

"See you around." Melony smiles, and having done as she intended, returns to Edwin's manor.

Ashli isn't one for celebration. She distances herself from them, but not far enough to miss their merriment, and sets her mind on the battles to come—and her hatred towards her mother.

A sword filled with anger and hatred will never reach me. An annoying phrase, tormenting Ashli's head.

"Hey," greets Kasen.

"What," she snaps, not evening turning to face him.

"I got so caught up with stuff over the past few days, I nearly forgot to give this to you." Kasen reveals the small round rusted shield.

Ashli stares blankly at it. "Are you mocking me?"

"Er. No? A lady asked me to give this to you. She said you still have a long way to go. Whatever that means."

"Hmph. She can take that ridiculous thing and shove it up her—" The shield disappears from Kasen's hands and reappears at Ashli's waist. *Even from far away, you ridicule me, Mother.*

"Guess she really wanted you to have it," chuckles Kasen.

"Don't you have anywhere else to be? Battle approaches and our allies waste time feasting when we should be preparing."

"Interesting how you say that," replies Kasen. "I think even you realize we can't win this battle without everyone doing their part. It's nice knowing that you at least consider us allies."

'*Something like that,*' she thinks. The two stood side-by-side, staring off into the horizon.

"Hey, super pal and companion! I want to stare dramatically into the horizon, too." Kika ruins the moment as she squeezes her way between them.

"Yeah. Quit hogging it for yourselves." Vonnie slides in next to Kasen, and the four of them watch the late afternoon sky.

"That was the best game of hide-n'-seek ever. You still suck at it, companion."

Printed in the United States
By Bookmasters